ONE HUNDRED REFLECTIONS

AN ASPEN COVE SMALL TOWN ROMANCE

KELLY COLLINS

BOOK NOOK PRESS

CHAPTER ONE

No good deed goes unpunished, but what about bad deeds? Some might call her selfish, but Elsa Buchanan considered herself resourceful. A mother couldn't wait around forever to have grandchildren. Desperate times called for desperate measures. That's why she poked holes in her son's condoms. Who knew she'd get a two-for-one deal, with both her son and daughter expecting little ones with their significant others? Her only hope was that she'd survive long enough to hold her babies' babies.

"Mom? Are you home?"

Beth knew she was home because her car was in the driveway. While her house was conveniently close to her pregnant daughter, it was too close for comfort.

"In here, sweetheart." Elsa pinched her pale cheeks and slicked on her favorite shade of rose lipstick.

Beth marched into the bathroom with her hands on her hips and a look of stubborn disappointment on her face. "Please tell me you don't have a date with Trenton Van der Veen."

Elsa smiled. "All right, I don't have a date with him." It wasn't really a date. It was a business transaction. The one thing Elsa was good at was reading people and Trenton Van der Veen was as slick as the just-polished surface of his Mercedes Benz. He wasn't really her type, but she was his. She was breathing and had a checkbook. If she played her cards right, she could smile pretty, flirt a little, and maybe bully him into a better deal. "It's a business dinner."

Beth narrowed her eyes. "What kind of business do you have with him?"

Elsa leaned toward the mirror and rubbed at the smudge below her eye. When it didn't come off, she realized how tired she was. She would do well to follow her own advice. Worry didn't change things, action did, and that was why she found herself living in Aspen Cove next to her daughter and a few blocks from her son.

"I'm buying the house Jewel Monroe and his son refurbished."

Beth's head rolled from side to side like a tilt-a-whirl. "But you live here."

It was so sweet that her daughter wanted her close by, but it wasn't convenient.

"Oh, honey. I love you, but there's close and then there's too close, and living next door is the latter. No mother wants to hear what's going on between the sheets of their kids."

"You can't hear us."

With a roll of her eyes, she said, "Unusually warm days." She turned and stared. "Windows open?"

"Oh. My. God. You listened?"

Elsa walked past her daughter and out of the bathroom. She went straight to her closet, where she perused the offerings. She really needed to get new clothes. Everything hanging in her closet screamed librarian, from the slacks and skirts to the sensible pumps. She rummaged through the rack and found a pair of black pants and paired them with a red and black shirt. Red was a power color. She let out a little bubble of laughter.

"What are you laughing about?" The one thing about Beth was she was as stubborn as an ox, and Elsa knew that she'd stand there until she got an answer. At least she wasn't asking the important questions just yet.

"I was thinking about the color red and how it's

deemed a power color." She giggled again. "I told Mr. Van der Veen to change his red tie because I would not be intimidated by his show of power."

Beth smiled. "And yet, you're going to wear red?"

Elsa shrugged. "Of course. I have to show him who's boss straight out of the gate."

"You know, Mom, you don't have to be in charge all the time."

That wasn't true. Every person was the captain of their ship. Controlling one's life meant making sure it didn't run aground or get lost at sea. Elsa Buchanan had been like Captain Blackbeard her entire life. She turned and steered herself in the right direction each time—even when a hurricane threatened. The one thing she knew was she couldn't throw her sails up and hope for wind. Sometimes, a woman had to create her own storm. It was in the center of that tempest where she could harness the power to survive.

"Oh, nonsense. There are followers and leaders."

Beth laughed. "And then there's you."

Elsa quickly undressed and redressed.

"What's that supposed to mean?"

Beth rubbed her swollen stomach. "You make your own rules."

Her daughter wasn't wrong. If she couldn't make the rules, then she simply changed the game. That's how she ended up becoming the soon-to-be grandmother of two babies due within a week of each other.

"I like rules." There was something comforting about them. "If I can make them, then why not?"

"Don't you ever get tired? I mean, you're always one step ahead of everyone else. That has to be exhausting."

"Better to be a step ahead than a mile behind."

"What are we even talking about?" Beth asked.

"How should I know? This is your conversation. Make the rules." She looked down at Beth's pregnant belly. "Pretty soon, you'll be a mom and you'll have to make lots of rules. Some for you and many for your kids."

"If you were my kid, I'd forbid you from going on a date with Mason's father."

Elsa walked out of the room and down the hallway into the living room.

"It's not a date."

"You're going to Trevi's Steakhouse. That's a date place."

She looked at her watch and saw she had about fifteen minutes before her "date" would get here, so she sat on the corner chair next to her newly installed bookshelves.

"It's the only place that serves a decent martini."

Beth flopped onto the oversized sofa. "Don't get sauced and let that man take advantage of you."

Since when did her daughter become the mother? She tapped her chin. Oh yeah, that must have been at about the time she got pregnant with Gray's baby.

"I don't need you to mother me."

Beth smiled. "Just practicing, Grandma." She used the name as if it were something negative.

Many women cringed at the grandma moniker, but Elsa looked forward to it. She was excited to open her life to new experiences and possibilities. All parents wanted was for their children to be independent and happy. She hit the lotto with Merrick and Beth. They were smart and capable and would make excellent parents. They chose wisely when it came to significant others. She considered that thought and shook her head. Neither chose wisely, but they got lucky. Merrick tried to pull the wool over her eyes when he brought Deanna home as his fake girlfriend. Beth had a moment of weakness for a musician. A one-night stand turned into a lifetime commitment.

"I'm excited to be a grandmother. I can't wait." That was an absolute truth.

"Obviously."

She let out a deep exhale. "I won't apologize. Look at where you're at. You are with an amazing man who loves you to the ends of the earth. You're pregnant with a beautiful baby who will change the lives of everyone. Who knows, maybe she'll be the next president."

"She could be he."

"True, and he'll be amazing as well." She hoped she got one of each—a boy from Merrick and a girl from Beth. Her child inside hoped her kids had children just like them. Merrick would get a pleasant old soul and Beth would get a hellion. It seemed only fitting.

"Back to this date." Beth frowned. "Don't forget I work for Jewel and she's with Mason, so I get inside information."

"Is that how you found out I was going to Trevi's with Trenton?"

She shook her head. "No, Maisey told me when I stopped for pie at the diner."

"Are there any secrets?"

"Not in a small town. If you don't want people to know something, you better hide it well."

Elsa's gut twisted. "Right." How long could she keep her kids in the dark?

A light tap sounded at the door.

"Looks like my date is here." She stood and walked to the door.

"Mom, is this a date or not?"

Elsa picked up her bag from the entry table and opened the door. Standing before her was Trenton, wearing a navy-blue suit and no tie. She loved a train-able man.

Looking over her shoulder at Beth, she smiled. "Don't wait up for me and lock the door on your way out."

Beth hopped up and marched toward them. "What time will you have my mother home?"

His eyes widened, and he turned to her.

"Pay her no mind, Trenton. She's practicing parenting. I'd say she's got the intimidation tactic down pat." She leaned toward Beth and gave her a kiss on the cheek. "Stop eating so much pie, it makes you testy."

She took Trenton's arm and let him lead her to his SUV. He let her go and walked to the driver's side, expecting her to continue to the passenger's side, but she stopped and waited at the closed door.

He glanced at her over the roof of the black vehicle.

"You're a handful, aren't you?"

"You have no idea."

He chuckled as he rounded the SUV and opened the door for her. "No, but I'm intrigued."

She took a seat and buckled in while he raced around to his door. Once seated and buckled in, he started the engine and backed out.

Inside, Elsa chuckled. Poor Trenton didn't have a

clue what he was in for. Calling her a handful was an understatement.

She thought back to her analogy of life and storms. She wasn't a gentle rain. She was a monsoon, and she often swept people away with her power. When it came to men, she needed a hurricane, and that's what Trenton Van der Veen was. The moment she met him, she felt the prickling of his power under her skin. Yes, she was a storm, but lately she was missing the spark she needed. He was most definitely a bolt of lightning. Unpredictable and unexpected.

She turned to face him. "Let me tell you how this is going to go."

He lifted a silver brow. "You already know?"

"Oh, yes. That's my superpower."

"Okay, Miss Buchanan. Tell me how my evening will unfold."

She wasn't usually so bold on a first encounter. Typically, she waited until a second meeting to outline the rules of engagement, but recent life developments required a change of plans.

"We'll have small talk, and then you'll agree to sell me the property for ten percent under asking price. You'll also give up your commission because six percent is ridiculous when the house sold itself."

He let out a full belly laugh. "Why would I do that?"

She smoothed her hair. "Because you're a man

who appreciates quality, and I'm quality. If you're lucky, I may even kiss you good night."

"Is that right?" He sat tall and straight, like a metal ruler. "I'm not used to getting so little."

She let out a *pffft* sound. "Darling," she reached out and set her hand on his arm, "you may get a lot, but you really shouldn't be shopping at the dollar store. You get what you pay for."

CHAPTER TWO

Trenton Van der Veen wasn't often surprised by people, but Elsa Buchanan was a surprise. She was full of vim and vigor and a good dose of sass. He liked that in a woman but hadn't found it in many.

"Did you say Trevi's Steakhouse?" he asked as he pulled out of the driveway.

She shifted in her seat to face him. She was a stunning woman with eyes the color of cornflowers and hair that wasn't quite brown, nor red, nor blonde. It was an eclectic mix of all three that seemed to fit her personality.

What little he knew of the woman told him she wasn't common.

"I hear it's the best that Copper Creek offers."

He scoffed. "That's not saying much. Have you

looked around? Outside of pine trees, ticks and the cove, there isn't much here."

She reached over and patted his arm. "I'm here and probably more than you can handle."

He chuckled, but knew she was right. He was a force to be reckoned with in the boardroom, but his social skills left a lot to be desired.

"What brings you to Aspen Cove?"

She moved in her seat like a worm. "I'm not sure I'm ready for the confessional."

He turned onto the highway and headed toward Copper Creek.

"I'm hardly qualified to absolve you."

She turned to face the dash and let out a sigh. "I impregnated both of my children."

He hit the brakes, sending them both hurtling forward until the safety belts caught them and yanked them back.

"You what?"

She rubbed at her shoulder. "That story will take a pricey glass of wine to get it out of me."

"I'm intrigued."

She smiled. "So you said."

"Without spilling all your secrets, tell me something about you."

"I have a passion for books."

He nodded. He, too, loved to read. He preferred the classics but had recently developed a Sci-fi Fantasy appetite. He plowed through Jules Verne and was diving into *Wheel of Time.*

"I also love to read. What are you enjoying currently?"

She opened her bag and pulled out *Pride and Prejudice,* holding it up and out so he could see it out of the corner of his eye.

"I'm a fan of the classics, but a good bodice ripper from time to time is a nice change of pace."

"It is a truth universally acknowledged, that a single man in possession of a good fortune, must be in want of a wife," he recited from memory.

"Jane Austen fan?"

"Who isn't?"

He caught her smile, and it warmed him.

"You don't come across as a romantic," she said.

He shook his head. There was a time when his entire being was filled with romance, but that died about six months after his marriage to Margaret when he found her with her lover.

"I think we all start out romantic, but life straightens that out mighty fast." He wound around the mountain road, taking in the scenery. He'd spent so much time building an empire, trying to fill the void in his heart, that he might have missed a lot of his life in the middle. Lately, he'd been thinking about his life and how it seemed two-dimensional. Almost losing Mason opened his eyes.

"Bitter man?"

He rocked his head back and forth. "Bitter? Probably, but ultimately, we are the captain of our ship and I steered mine aground long ago." He smiled. "I'm just getting a little wind in my sails once again. What about you?"

She tucked her book back into her bag. "Oh, I'm not looking for love." She patted the leather. "I've got Mr. Darcy for that. All I'm looking for right now is a nice dinner, and an exceptional deal on my new home."

"You forgot the kiss."

She laughed. "That isn't a given, Mr. Van der Veen. My kisses have to be earned."

He pulled into the parking lot of Trevi's and turned off the engine. "Shall we start with a glass of wine, then?"

He exited the car and saw that she waited for him to open her door. He liked a woman who wasn't afraid to demand what she wanted. Obviously, Elsa wanted him to be chivalrous—maybe a modern-day Mr. Darcy.

He opened the door and held out his hand, which she took until she stood. They walked together with his hand on the small of her back into the restaurant, where he asked for a private table near the window.

They were led to the corner table with a view of

a canyon. The setting sun cast an orange glow on the red rocks, making them seem like they were ablaze.

"Beautiful," she said.

He stared at her. "Yes, you are."

She smiled. "Flattery will get you nowhere, Mr. Van der Veen."

It was his turn to smirk. "Oh, in my experience, it gets you everywhere."

She pulled her napkin from the table and set it on her lap. "We'll see."

The server approached and took their drink order. As she warned, Elsa ordered a glass of very expensive wine. He wouldn't have cared if she'd ordered the bottle. He enjoyed watching her try to unsettle him. She did, but not in the way she thought. He was already going to give her a good deal on the house. He didn't need to make a profit on the Aspen Cove homes. They were a learning lesson for his son, although in the end he ended up learning a lesson of his own.

He'd spent decades hanging onto a marriage that didn't work because he refused to fail, and in the end, he failed at everything. He had buried himself in his work and his masseuse to ease the pain and to fill the hollows. It didn't work. He had only alienated his son, made his soon-to-be ex-wife miserable, and he turned into the man he didn't want to be—a modern day Scrooge.

"What do you recommend?" he asked her as soon as the server was gone.

She opened the menu. "I've never been here." Her eyes traversed the menu. "Everything looks good."

He didn't bother looking at his menu, but flagged the server over and asked for him to bring them a variety of the restaurant's most popular offerings. Seeing a substantial tip in his future, the waiter hightailed it out of there, probably so Trenton couldn't change his mind.

"All of that? How are we supposed to eat so much?"

He glanced out the window and saw the flame orange sky fade into a pumpkin glow. How had he missed so much beauty in the world? He had a lot to make up for in his life, and he was starting now.

"I'm a fierce negotiator," he said. "We could be here for hours." He took his napkin and laid it across his lap. "What we don't eat for dinner, we can have for breakfast."

Her perfectly-plucked brows arched. "Let me assure you, Mr. Van der Veen. I'm not easy."

Laughter bubbled up inside him. He tried to contain it, but it burst free. When he calmed down, he looked at her and said, "That's apparent. Where do you want to start?"

The waiter dropped off the wine and a charcu-terie tray.

She lifted her glass. "How about a toast?"

"To?" he asked as he raised his glass.

"The classics, whether it be books, homes, or manners."

He tapped her glass. "To a twenty-first century woman with a nineteenth century heart."

She sipped her wine, and he could see the plea-sure on her face as the liquid washed over her taste-buds. She was so expressive that he could almost taste it through her experience. He had to admit that having money had its perks and buying quality wine was one of them.

"So, tell me, Trenton,"—she licked her lips like she was tasting his name on them—"if they cast you in *Pride and Prejudice,* who would you be?"

He was taken aback by the question because he wasn't one character but a bit of all of them.

He considered his answer for a long moment. "While I'm fairly certain you'd like me to say Mr. Darcy, I'm not sure that's me."

She moved her glass in a circle until the deep red washed up the sides. "Oh, not surly and difficult and hard to please?"

He didn't expect that either. He expected her to romanticize the character. "Oh, I'm all that, but I wouldn't say that I've ever been the one to swoop in and save the day."

She lowered her head but looked at him through the sweep of her hair. "Oh, I don't know. You saved Jewel, or so I hear."

His eyes widened. "I wouldn't call it that. I simply righted a wrong and gave her and my son a choice."

She forked a bite of cheese and brought it to her lips. "Choices are today's aphrodisiac."

He forked a bite of salami and offered it to her. "Well, by all means, indulge."

She gave him a coy smile. "Oh, I plan to. Now, back to the question. Who are you?"

He settled into his seat while she ate his offering and waited for his reply. "I'm all the characters. I've been a Wickham and a Bingley and, regrettably, a Collins at times. I've even been an Elizabeth Bennet. No one is a single personality but an amalgamation of them all. The beauty of the book is that you connect with every character." He let his eyes roll to the ceiling. "Except for Mrs. Bennet. I don't get her at all."

She grabbed a green olive. "You're not a woman with daughters."

"Very true. What's next on your list?"

She sat up and her eyes lit up. "I'm reading the hundred books you should read before you die."

"As a lover of books, I would have imagined you'd already read them."

"Twice. I might have forgotten to mention I was a librarian for thirty years."

His eyes grew wide. "Twice? Once is enough for some of them, but twice would kill me."

She seemed to soften and sink into her chair. "We all have to die someday, and when I do, I want my headstone to read, *She read them all and lived.*"

Dish after dish came out from calamari to tuna tartar, steak Dianne to lobster mac and cheese, and all the while they talked books and movies. Hands down, they both thought the books were always more entertaining.

It was over dessert that they started their negotiations. He would not give in easily, even though he knew he'd give in. Elsa seemed to be the type of woman who had to fight for everything. He didn't know if that was by design or not, but he wouldn't allow her to feel like he'd given in. Something told him she was a formidable opponent, and the win would be more important to her than to him.

"You know the house faces west, which means I'll have ice problems in the winter."

She was negotiating by inconvenience.

"Then buy another house." He finished his wine and asked for a cup of coffee.

"But I like that one. It's open and airy. I don't feel

trapped like I do at the place I'm living in now, which is dark and cave-like."

He'd learned over his years of doing business that words were incredibly important, and a connoisseur of words probably chose them wisely. Elsa didn't like feeling confined.

"It has been remodeled by a professional with a following. That is worth something."

She waved him off. "You know those shows cut corners. They are on a timeline and often can't pay attention to the details."

He had to give her credit because her arguments weren't cookie cutter. They were as unique as she was.

"What's your best offer?"

She sat for an extended period as if she were calculating everything in her head.

"I won't pay over eighty percent of what you're asking."

The waiter arrived with the coffee, and in Trenton's attempt to take it, he almost tipped it over.

"Are you kidding?" he asked in an incredulous voice. "Just hours ago, you offered me ten percent below asking price."

She cleared her throat and gave him a stern librarian look. The kind that could send a kid scurrying into the stacks for cover.

"That was before I realized how much work

you'd be." She smiled. "I mean, how much work the house would take." She swept her hand dramatically across her forehead. "Did you not hear me tell you I'm a bibliophile? I'll need built-ins for my collection. There's so much work to be done."

"I heard you." He'd heard everything. She saw him as a project. While that might have rubbed him wrong in the past, he was looking for an adventure. Elsa Buchanan was going to be one wild ride.

They settled for twelve percent below asking price and he'd have her bookshelves installed.

By the time they got back to Aspen Cove, and he walked her to the door, he was half in love with her already. She was a force to be reckoned with—an earthquake he wasn't expecting. She was seven point eight on the Richter scale and she knocked him off-balance, but he was no minor tremor either. It was time to move and shake Elsa's world, too.

"I'll bring by the paperwork tomorrow." He handed her the bag of leftovers.

She set it down and ran her hand up the front of his shirt until she got to the top button. "About that kiss?"

He smiled and stepped back. "I may be cheap, but I'm not easy." He turned and walked away to the sound of her laughter.

CHAPTER THREE

Her doctor in Denver called her a closet hypochondriac because she insisted she had breast cancer. He told her it was all in her head. That the tiny pea-sized lump she felt wasn't a thing to worry about. She believed him until months later it had grown into a bean-sized lump. He said her latest mammogram showed a mass, but he was certain it was a fluid-filled cyst. He'd seen them a thousand times.

She fired him that day. A woman knows her body, and Elsa knew the lump in her right breast wasn't normal. Why did men always think they knew better?

She looked around the drab living room of her daughter's home. It had good bones, but needed a lot of work. Not even the bookshelves she had built could bring light into the place with the colorful bindings that graced the shelves. Nope, this place needed light, the kind that came from bay windows and skylights and funny men.

She was still giggling when she woke up that morning. Trenton leaving her on the porch after telling her he was cheap just tickled her funny bone. She needed a good laugh, and he provided it.

She picked up her keys and walked out the door. She had an appointment with Dr. Parker before meeting Trenton at the diner to go over the paperwork.

As she drove down the street, a feeling of dread washed over her. What if her time was really running out?

It was an impulsive move to poke holes in her son's condoms. Call it woman's intuition or whatever you like, but her son was taking too long to get what she wanted—a grandchild. And the lump? She found out it wasn't cancerous, but her new doctor wanted to watch it. Maybe Elsa was a closet hypochondriac, and the fact that it had doubled in size again was nothing.

She parked in front of the bakery and got out of her car, lifting her nose into the air to smell the brownies Katie was baking. That girl was single-handedly responsible for the five pounds she'd gained since moving to town.

With a few minutes to spare, she detoured into B's Bakery for a treat. In her fifty-plus years of experience, chocolate was the panacea for whatever ailed her.

The bell above the door rang and from the back-room, a little blonde ball of fire ran out to greet her.

"Welcome to B's," the girl said. Her hair was pulled into pigtails and her mouth was ringed with chocolate.

"Sahara Bishop, you get back here now!" Katie walked out of the back room drying her hands on her apron. "Good morning, Elsa. I see you've met my little racoon." She winked. "Most have dark rings around their eyes, but mine has one around her mouth because she snuck into the chocolate chips while her mommy wasn't paying attention."

She pointed to Sahara and then crooked her finger in a "come here" manner.

"She's the official greeter." Elsa bent over and scooped Sahara up. She had to be close to three, give or take a little.

"When she can make change and mix cookies, I'll hire her."

Elsa carried her to her mom and handed her off. "She's got one major ingredient down."

Katie smiled at her daughter and Elsa could see

how much Sahara meant to her mom. There was no substitution for a mother's love or the unconditional love of a child.

Soon, Elsa's son and daughter would both have children, and they'd experience that gift firsthand.

"I just pulled some brownies from the oven. They're your favorite, right?"

Elsa tapped her nose. "They are what brought me in."

"Let me get you a couple from the back. Those are still warm." She tugged on one pigtail. "Let's call Daddy and tell him you're ready to go fishing."

There was a squeal of excitement as Katie took Sahara into the back.

While Elsa waited, she looked around the bakery, her eyes stopping on The Wishing Wall. It was a novel idea. She knew Katie did her best to grant the wishes she could. Cookies for a birthday. Date night with a loved one. Clothes. Food. Money.

Elsa had never filled out a sticky note. It was her belief that whatever she needed, she'd provide. Not once had anyone come through for her. Life had been something she had to wrestle with her entire existence, so the concept of wishing for something and having it happen was as foreign as the thought of eating bugs instead of brownies. However, she was trying new things these days. Given her current state of "hypochondria" she could use a little magic, so she peeled a yellow Post-it note and wrote her wish.

It was a simple request because Elsa believed in having attainable goals. If this one worked out for her, she'd be a regular visitor to the wall.

She folded it up and used a thumbtack to affix it to the corkboard.

"Here you go," Katie said as she came from the back. "Sorry it took so long, but Bowie came by to get the baby." She held up a bag that was embellished with the simple B's Bakery logo. "I gave you a double helping since you waited so long."

Elsa smiled and walked over to the corkboard to take down her note.

"Hey," Katie said. "I haven't looked at that one yet." She rang her up and handed her the bag with the brownie.

"Wish granted. I asked for a big brownie." Maybe there was something to that wall after all. "How did you know?"

"I'm magical that way." Katie laughed. "Or I felt bad about keeping you waiting. You choose."

"I'll stick with magical." Elsa handed over a few bills and told her to keep the change. "Have a good day."

"You too," Katie said.

With her bag in her hand, she crossed the street

and walked into the building with the flashing light in the window that said "The Doctor is in."

Agatha was behind the counter, eating popcorn and watching Jeopardy.

Elsa had never considered the game show popcorn-worthy television.

"I'm here to see Dr.—"

Agatha held up her hand. "It's the last question. The category is authors, and the question is: In 1937 his sister said he had 'hats of every description,' which he would use as the foundation of his next book."

The music played as the contestants wrote their answers.

"Do you know it?" Elsa asked.

"Haven't got a clue." Agatha shook her head and grumbled.

"Dr. Seuss," Elsa answered.

"No, it's Parker or Covington."

Elsa laughed. "No, the answer is Dr. Seuss. But I'm here to see Dr. Parker."

Agatha gave her a perplexed look. "How did you know?"

"The answer, or the doctor I have an appointment with?" They were talking in circles, but by Agatha's dumbfounded expression they were finally on the same page. "I have lots of useless information stored in my brain from thirty years as a public librarian."

"I'd say." Agatha popped a pinch of popcorn into her mouth. "Follow me," she said around the bite.

Down the hallway, they walked until they got to a door on the right, which Agatha knocked on and opened.

Inside stood Dr. Covington.

"Come on in." She pointed to a gown on the table. "You change and I'll step out."

Elsa was a bit confused. "I'm supposed to see Dr. Parker."

Lydia chuckled. "Oh, you will. He's given up boobs and below the belt for women."

Agatha let out a hoot. "That's what he'd like you to believe, but he likes mine just fine."

Doc's voice carried from down the hallway. "Don't be telling my secrets, Agatha. Don't you have work to do?"

The older woman's cheeks pinked, and she dashed away.

Five minutes later, Elsa was alone with Dr. Lydia Covington.

"I can see why you're concerned."

After an exaggerated exhale, she said, "I've been told twice it's nothing. Deep inside I know it's something."

Lydia leaned against the counter. "I think we should get it biopsied."

"You do?" While that sounded scary, it also sounded wise. That's all she wanted from the start.

"I think we have an internal voice that tells us when something isn't right. If you've got an alarm going off, we have a few choices. We could choose to keep the path and hope it's nothing and your alarm shuts off automatically, or we can listen to it and see if it's alerting us to a problem."

Her insides vibrated, but Elsa wasn't sure if that was nerves or her body celebrating. Often women aren't taken seriously, and in the end, they pay the price.

"Thank you. I just need to know."

The knocking on the door had both women turning their heads. "It's just me," Doc said as he shuffled in. "What have we got?"

Lydia told him of her findings.

He rubbed at his mustache and frowned, then wrote the name and number of a doctor in Copper Creek on a note.

"You call Dr. Roberta Trendle. She'll hook you up."

"Is she an oncologist?"

Doctor Parker shook his head. "Now listen here." He picked up the pen and tapped it on the counter. "We don't need a cancer specialist until we've found out it's cancer. Until then, we're going to assume it's nothing."

She pressed her hand to her gown-covered breast. "But it's something. I can feel something."

He nodded. "I understand that, and we won't make light of it, or dismiss it, but we won't give it life until we have to."

"You're right." She knew worrying was useless, but she couldn't help it. "I've got two grandbabies on the way."

He made a whistling sound as he sucked his teeth. "Should I hide the condoms on display when you're in the store? You're responsible for more than half the pregnant women in town."

She hung her head. "Not my proudest moment, but I wouldn't change a thing."

He smiled. "I know. Charlie had twins and those boys are the highlight of my life. They'll be more interesting when they do something other than eat and poop."

"I can't wait."

"Well, you'll have to, but until then, keep yourself busy. Idle minds are dangerous."

"If you had a library, I'd volunteer. I'm helping at the bookstore when I can, but Natalie and Jake seem to have that under control."

Doc smiled. It was a calculated smile that told Elsa she was in for something big.

"We need a historian." He cleared his throat. "We've got Tilden Cool, but he was really just trying to find out about himself when he dug up all the stuff on the townsfolk. What we need is someone to make sense of everything we have. Maybe someday, we can have a museum of sorts." He nodded. "You're perfect." He got up and walked toward the door.

"But—"

"You can thank me later. I'll have everything we've got delivered to your house—your new one."

She was taken aback. "How did you know?"

He touched his ear. "They keep growing. I think it's so we can hear better."

Lydia threw the pen he left on the counter at him. "You only hear what you want to hear."

Doc leaned in. "What was that?"

Lydia rubbed her temples. "Exactly."

As soon as the door was closed, Lydia took out her phone and called Dr. Trendle directly. By the end of the conversation, Elsa had an appointment for the end of the following week.

By the time she was dressed and out the door with her jumbo brownie in hand, she was late to her meeting with Trenton.

When she walked inside, she found him in a booth to the right next to the jukebox.

"You're late." He stood as she walked over.

She looked at her wrist as if there was a watch there. "Am I?"

He waited for her to be seated before he took his seat again.

"You are."

She smiled. "Don't worry, I'm worth the wait."

CHAPTER FOUR

"So am I." Last night, he told her he wasn't easy, and that was true. He wasn't easy. Many would call him a piece of work; most would call him an asshole, including his own son, but people don't get to where they are without the help of others, and he had many molding his life from a young age.

She held up a bag. "I bought us a brownie."

He eyed the bag from B's Bakery. It was one of his favorite stops, too, but he had a soft spot for the cranberry orange muffins they made on Tuesdays.

"Don't let Maisey see that when she has the best pies in town."

She looked around like a child trying to sneak a cookie from the jar and slipped the bag into her purse.

"Keep my secret?"

"Only if you share later."

She smiled. He loved a woman's smile, but not every woman could light a room with hers. Elsa Buchanan was like a hundred-watt bulb in a pitch-black room.

"Deal, but you have to buy me pie." She pulled the menu from the stand.

"Is that all you want?" He'd seen her eat last night, and she wasn't someone who nibbled. She had a hardy appetite, but he figured it took a lot of energy to keep that sass going. He'd be glad to feed it all day long.

"Oh no." She perused the menu for a moment and then put it down. "I'll have the patty melt and fries." She tapped her chin. "But onion rings sound good too. Hmm."

Maisey sauntered up. The squeak of her sensible loafers against the checkerboard floor stopped when she did.

"Hey kids, what can I get ya?"

He looked at Elsa. "You first."

"No, you go." She was obviously still debating, so he figured he'd take some of the pressure off. "Grilled cheese and fries… and a side of onion rings," he said. "Oh, and a diet soda."

Maisey laughed. "You think that will help?"

He lifted his shoulders. "Can't hurt."

She scribbled his order on her pad and looked at
Elsa.

"I'll have the patty melt and fries and a chocolate
malt."

Maisey wrote the order and raised a brow.
"Should I add in a side of vascular surgery?"

"Hey, you called us kids," he said. "That means
we're invincible."

"They think, until the first creak of arthritis kicks
in." Maisey rolled her neck and Trenton heard every
pop of her vertebrae. "I'll get that order in."

"Chocolate malt, eh?"

She rocked her head back and forth. "It was a
toss-up between chocolate and strawberry, but I figured I could get my fruit fix with a piece of cherry
pie."

He stared at her for a moment. She wasn't a large
woman by any means. Some might even call her thin.
"Where do you put it all?" He knew he'd be full after
half of his meal, and he was twice her size.

She kicked out her leg and raised it to show jeans
and a pair of white sneakers. "Hollow leg."

"Can you buy one of those or do they come with
the original equipment?" he teased.

She laughed. "Oh, this girl's nearly an antique,
and it's all original equipment. You don't find them
like this anymore."

That was for darn sure. All he found were treasure hunters and freebie seekers. That was fine if you knew what you were in for. He internally chuckled because Elsa was right when she told him he got what he paid for.

"You're right. Everything is new, but how do you improve on a classic? Sometimes it's better to leave perfection alone." He smiled at her, but he was certain she didn't see a hundred-watt bulb in his grin. The people of Aspen Cove were programmed to see him as a villain. He couldn't blame them. He'd done a lot of wrong everywhere, including Aspen Cove. He planned to fix what he could and file the rest under lessons learned.

They say you can't teach an old dog new tricks, but that wasn't true. What this old dog needed to learn was that change was good and perspective was personal.

"Shall we get started?" he asked.

She wiggled in her seat. "Yes, I'm excited."

"First time homeowner?"

She made a sound something like *pffft* and waved her hand in the air. "This isn't my first rodeo, but it will be my last."

"Planning on staying in Aspen Cove?"

"I don't plan on leaving."

He wasn't sure he liked that, considering his life was in Denver. There weren't any nearby golf courses or country clubs in Aspen Cove. And while

Trevi's was nice, it wasn't Ellyngton's at the Brown Palace. They didn't have a decent ramen house and sushi wasn't an option unless he went back to Denver. The only thing Aspen Cove had going for it was his son, Mason, and Elsa Buchanan.

"That's right, you impregnated your children. Care to tell me about that?"

She turned cherry pie red. "I told you that will take wine. You missed your window of opportunity last night."

He picked up the folder sitting on the bench beside him and placed it on the table between them.

"I'm always a day late and a dollar short."

"Somehow I don't believe you."

Maisey swung by and dropped off their drinks.

"You might want to eat first before you do business." She stared straight at him and gave him a look that warned him to be nice. "I hear real estate can cause indigestion."

Elsa smiled up at her. "How did you know?"

Maisey tossed her head back. "Small town, honey. If you can't get all the gossip from the diner, you go to Cove Cuts. Marina has a good ear." She palmed the curl of her bob. "She does a great job on my hair too."

"Don't believe everything you hear." Trenton took a sip of his soda and realized how that came out.

"I mean, your hair looks amazing, but I'm not the bad guy."

Maisey pointed a finger at him. "Walks like a duck, talks like a duck, probably a duck."

He shook his head. "I'm a swan, and I'll prove it."

She spun around to leave, but looked over her shoulder. "A good tip will help. I've got a grandbaby on the way." She bolted from their table like her skirt was on fire.

"Did you get her kid pregnant too?"

Elsa turned white. "I hope not, but I suppose it's possible."

He shook his head. "You're a menace to the town."

She hung her head. "I'm pretty sure you're right."

He let the subject drop for now, but he wouldn't forever. There was a story there, and he was certain it would be a side-splitting one.

He opened the folder where all the papers were in order. It was a quit claim deed, since she'd already wired the money to his office. All that was left was about two dozen signatures, and the house was hers.

She looked over the contract and smiled.

"You even put the bookshelves in here."

"I'm thorough."

She picked up her glass and sucked through the straw. The shake must have been thick, because her cheeks hollowed out before she closed her eyes and smiled.

"When I was pregnant with Merrick, I had one of these a day. There's something about malt that's so satisfying."

"Were you as big as a house when you delivered?" He wanted to take the words back as soon as they were out. But they were already out there.

He expected Elsa to look indignant, but she didn't. She chuckled and took another drink.

"Size of a two-story with a mother-in-law suite in the back, but I didn't care. He was the most beautiful baby."

He stared at her for a long moment. "When my wife had Mason, she held herself to a strict twelve hundred calories a day. When he was born, he looked like a shar pei, all skin and bones." He rubbed his smooth chin. "She left him with a nanny for a month while she went to a slimming spa."

Her eyes grew wide. "At twelve hundred calories a day, she was probably thinner than she was when you got her pregnant." She cocked her head. "Did you say wife?" Her eyes narrowed. "And you were going to kiss me." She growled from deep in her throat. "You are a Wickham."

He should have been offended, but he wasn't. "I told you I've been all of them."

She held up a finger. "Except Mrs. Bennet."

"True, I'm not a shrew. As for my wife, she's a recent ex-wife, and it's difficult to get used to the change."

"Still pining for her?"

Maisey arrived with the meal and placed the onion rings in the center. She pulled a ketchup bottle from her pocket and several extra napkins. That pocket was like the carpet bag from *Mary Poppins*. Trenton was certain if Elsa asked for a water, Maisey would reach inside and pull out a glass with ice.

"Oh, no." He vigorously shook his head. "That marriage was over as soon as it began. But it took thirty years to end it."

"Why so long?" She took the ketchup and squeezed a puddle on her plate.

"I'm not a quitter, and I don't like to lose."

"But you cheated." Her statement was fact, not accusation.

"Umm." He tilted his head back and thought of an acceptable way to justify his actions, but there wasn't one. "I did. I'm not justifying anything, but my ex-wife," he put emphasis on ex, "she fell in love at the slimming spa with her trainer."

"Oh." She dragged her fry through the ketchup. "Go on." She leaned in like she was watching the best part of a movie.

"I tried to win back her love, but she told me I never had it to start. Turns out she was interested in marrying the name, not the man." Years ago, that would've hurt to confess, but now it was old news. "Anyway, after ten years of celibacy, I strayed."

She picked up her patty melt and took a bite.

He could see the wheels spinning in her head from the way her eyes shifted.

"I was the other woman once," she said once she swallowed. "I didn't know it at the time. I thought he was single."

Trenton held both of his hands up like he was surrendering. "I've been nothing but honest with the women I saw."

She smiled. "Admirable given your reputation."

He took a bite of his sandwich and chewed on it and her words.

"Have you ever passed up something you thought would be good just because someone said they didn't like it?"

"I'm sure I have."

He ate an onion ring and continued. "Do you regret not deciding for yourself?"

She sat thoughtfully for a moment. "What I don't know, I can't regret." She smiled. "And sweetbreads sounded gross to begin with, so I trusted Mary Anne Whatley when she said to pass on the bull balls."

He'd taken a drink of his soda and choked on it. "You make me laugh."

"That's because I have a wicked sense of humor."

"Yes, you do."

They spent the rest of the meal talking about real estate in Colorado. By the time they ordered and ate their pie, the paperwork was complete, and Elsa owned the property on Hyacinth.

She stole it from him, but he was glad to offer it. His whole life he gave and his ex took. The last few years he felt like a dog protecting a bone, so to give freely without expectation felt amazing.

He pulled out a hundred-dollar bill and sat it on the table. "Shall we go see your house?"

"Are you leaving her that big a tip?"

He slid from the booth and helped her stand. "She's got a grandbaby on the way."

The light in Elsa's eyes twinkled. "Hey, I've got two. What do I get?"

He chuckled. "A bottle of wine so I can hear that story."

CHAPTER FIVE

Elsa stood on the front porch, key in hand, as Trenton watched her unlock the door. Why her hands trembled, she couldn't say, but they shook like a leaf in the wind.

Maybe it was because this was a new beginning, or maybe because there was a possibility that this might be the end.

"Are you going to stand there all day or are you going to open the door and step into the rest of your life?"

"Don't rush me," she said. "All good things come to those who wait."

He chuckled. "Sure, but I'd rather not need a walker by the time you enter."

She turned the key and walked inside. The house

smelled like furniture polish and freshly cut wood. It also smelled like home.

"You removed all the staging décor already?"

He came up behind her and stood so close she could feel the heat from his body.

"This is your house, and it should have your things." He moved to the long wall in the living room. "Is this where you want the shelves?"

She shook her head. "No, I'd like to have them go from floor to ceiling on the sides of the fireplace." She imagined her collection and all the colored bindings that would bring life and warmth to the space.

"That's a lot of books."

She'd been collecting books since she was a kid. While other girls collected *Teen Beat Magazine,* she bought *Anne of Green Gables* and *The Swiss Family Robinson.*

"I have an extensive collection."

"I'd love to see it."

She turned to him. He had a lost boy look in his eyes. Trenton Van der Veen wasn't a bad man. He was a man who'd made poor decisions, the first being his choice of wife.

"Are you planning on sticking around Aspen Cove?"

He looked at her thoughtfully before stepping into her personal space and thumbing her chin, so it tilted to look at him.

"Depends."

She cocked her head to the side.

"On what?"

He moved closer. "This." He pressed his lips to hers. It was a sweet soft kiss at first, but it turned into more.

She wasn't into the sloppy kisses teens snuck in the library alcoves, but when his tongue slipped past her lips, a jolt of excitement rushed all the way to her toes. She leaned into him and relished the warmth of his body and the sweet taste of his kiss.

He pulled away far too soon, and stood back, silent but watching.

"Yep, I'm sticking around." He shifted and moved toward the door. "I'll see you soon, Elsa."

She watched as he stepped out of the house and walked to his car.

"How soon?" She called after him, but all she heard was a chuckle before he put his vehicle in reverse and drove away.

"I STILL DON'T UNDERSTAND why you moved." Beth unpacked and placed the books on Elsa's newly-installed shelves.

"I love you, sweetie." She brushed her hand against Beth's cheek as she walked past. "But I need my space as well. Living next door to you was like having you in the basement."

Beth gasped. "What was wrong with me living in the basement?"

Elsa sighed and flopped into the overstuffed chair she'd placed in the corner. It was the perfect reading nook.

"Nothing. It was practical but not private." She lifted a brow. "You know, I can hear everything. I've told you before, install air conditioning. That way, the neighbors don't have to hear too."

"Mother." Beth's cheeks heated and turned as red as an overripe strawberry. "You can't possibly hear us and even if you could, you shouldn't listen."

Elsa laughed. "I'd need noise canceling headphones to drown out those sounds. Geez, are you hurting him?"

"You did not just ask me that." Beth shoved a handful of books onto the shelf.

"Hey, be careful. Some of those are first editions." She knew none of the ones her daughter placed were because she'd carefully unpacked those books herself.

"Speaking of first editions, I had my checkup with Lydia today, and everything looks good. She asked how you were feeling? Are you okay?"

Elsa wasn't ready to discuss her health issues with her kids because she wasn't certain she had a health issue. It had been over a week since she'd seen Lydia. Her appointment with Dr. Trendle was tomorrow.

"Sure, honey, why wouldn't I be?" Why wouldn't she be indeed? She hadn't told the kids her concerns. They had other stuff to worry about. Merrick was protecting a community and taking care of Deanna, who was creating a baby. Beth was feeding the community by watching over The Corner Store and incubating a little one as well.

"It was just the way she asked." Beth rubbed her lower back. "Kind of like she was following up on a visit."

Elsa dismissed it with a shrug. "It's her job to ask, but as far as I know, I'm fine." And that was the truth. "I'll be in Copper Creek tomorrow. Do you need anything?"

"Can I go with? I've got a list for the baby's room."

Elsa regretted letting her trip to Copper Creek out of the bag, but she knew if she disappeared without telling anyone, she'd be in trouble. It was as if the tables had turned, and she was now the child, and her kids, the parents. They kept a close eye on her, or the town did, and tattled.

"Not this time."

Beth placed her hands on her hips. "Why not?"

"Because this is a solo trip. I've got..." She had to

come up with an excuse as to why she didn't want her daughter along. "I've got a waxing appointment."

Beth's face twisted. "What are you waxing?"

Elsa loved how her kids thought that once she had reached fifty, she was on the shelf for life. She wasn't completely hip, but she wasn't left in the stone age either.

She widened her eyes and gave her daughter a do-you-really-want-to-know look. "It's not my legs."

Beth's hands went to her ears and then eyes and back to her ears. "I don't want to know."

Elsa pushed out of the chair. "Then don't ask."

"Fine." Beth collapsed the empty box. "I'm happy to see you're not dating Mr. Van der Mean."

"It's Van der Veen," she corrected.

"I know, but my version is fitting." Beth walked to the chair Elsa had vacated and took a seat. "He's not a nice man."

"He's a very nice man." Something in her wanted to defend Trenton. She hadn't heard from him since he left, but that kiss still lingered in her memory. "And a good kisser," she said without thinking.

"Mom! You did not kiss him."

Elsa walked into the kitchen and took a club soda from the refrigerator. "Okay, I didn't." She wasn't going to argue.

"Well, did you?" Beth leaned back and placed her hands on her stomach. Her rounded belly seemed to grow every day. At the halfway point, she had some growing to do, but Elsa had to admit that her daughter glowed from pregnancy.

"Did I what?" Now it was just a game they were playing.

"Kiss Mr. Van der Mean."

Elsa shook her head. "No, but I kissed Trenton Van der Veen, and it was nice."

Beth's lips formed a thin line which stayed that way until her next big inhale. "Geez, Mom, you can't just kiss all the men in town."

That made Elsa laugh so hard she was certain she'd pee her pants. "I'll have you know, he's the first man I've kissed in years."

"See, then, you have little to go on. You need to kiss a few more before you decide his is nice. I don't like eggplant but if I hadn't eaten in a while, let's say … years, it would seem like the best thing ever."

Elsa took a sip of her soda and then held up her hand. "Wait a minute. In one breath, you tell me I can't kiss all the men in town and then in the next you tell me to kiss more. What is it? You know, you'll have to be clear on your directives when you become a parent. Mixed messages can lead to disaster."

Beth narrowed her eyes with a harrumph. "Stop mothering me while I'm trying to mother you."

Elsa waved her off. "Please, like I need advice from a woman who borrows her brother's condoms."

Her mouth dropped open. "I've never."

"That isn't true." Elsa pointed at her rounded belly. "Anyway, I can take care of myself, but I'm touched that you're concerned. As for Trenton ... I haven't seen him since he left but I'm hopeful."

"Mom," Beth said in warning.

"He's a good man. You'll see. My arsehole meter has improved since your father."

"Let's hope."

A loud knock at the door made both women jump.

Elsa answered it to find Lloyd Dawson on her doorstep holding a large box.

He bowed his Stetson-covered head. "Elsa."

"Oh, Lloyd. Come on in."

He peeked inside as if he'd never been invited into a home before and, after a few seconds, he stomped his boots on the porch and stepped over the threshold.

He lifted the box. "I hear you're going to be the town historian." He nodded to the contents, which appeared to be a mishmash of pictures and papers. "I've had these in the attic for decades."

"Town historian?" Beth asked. "Well look at you, finding your perfect match." She looked at Lloyd, who seemed to blush. "I meant her hobby." Beth rocked until she got enough momentum to get to her feet. "I'll be going now." She passed Lloyd. "See you later, Mr. Dawson." She turned to Elsa and smiled. "Try that one."

Elsa closed the door. "Can I get you something to drink?"

He shook his head. "No, ma'am."

Elsa pointed to the coffee table. "You can set that over there." She wasn't expecting people to bring her their boxes of memories, but she supposed she had to start somewhere and she needed to distract her thoughts, which were focused on two things: cancer and Trenton.

Lloyd set the box down and stepped back toward the door. He seemed to hem and haw.

"Have you eaten?" he asked.

She had grabbed a muffin on the way over from the old house.

"Are you asking me on a date?"

Lloyd's face turned ashen. "Oh no, ma'am. I'm ... I'm ..."

She smiled and put a hand on his arm. "You're off the hook." She glanced behind her at the box. "It looks like I've got my work cut out for me, anyway."

He smiled. "If I was dating, you'd be my first choice, but I'm still ..."—sadness filled his eyes—"fig-uring things out. I'm close but not there."

"I understand. Thanks for the box." She opened the door to find Trenton standing there. He looked at her and then at Lloyd.

"Sorry," Trenton said. "I should have called."

Elsa recognized that look of jealousy on Trenton's face. To say she wasn't a little miffed at him for not calling was an understatement. He had nothing to be jealous of but was glaring at her like she was cheating and if she was going to be accused, if only by a look, then she might as well be guilty.

She turned to Lloyd and gripped the top of his shirt, pulling him down so she could kiss him. Not a passionate kiss, but a quick lip lock that was over before it began. Not a single spark ignited.

That wasn't true. She saw the fireworks explode from the top of Trenton's head.

"Thanks for everything, Lloyd. I love the gift."

The flustered man stumbled out the door and walked silently to his car.

Trenton stepped inside and shut the door. "I'm gone less than two weeks and you've replaced me?"

CHAPTER SIX

He wasn't sure how to feel about what he just witnessed. The glint in Elsa's eyes said she was messing with him but the twist in his gut warned him ... no, begged him to turn around and leave.

He was halfway to turning around when she reached out and touched his arm.

"You're hardly replaceable." She moved to the kitchen lightning fast. "What about a coffee?"

He looked around the house and was shocked to see how much had transpired since he'd left.

"You're fully moved in?"

She nodded. "I've got all my things, but not everything is unpacked yet."

She held up a coffee pod and a mug. "Are you

staying or going?" She lifted her eyes in a way that made her brows reach for her hairline.

He pondered her question for a moment. "Why did you kiss Lloyd?"

She turned her back on him and put the pod in the coffeemaker and pressed start. Within seconds, the air filled with the aroma of espresso and a hint of her perfume, which smelled like vanilla and brown sugar. It was the perfect mix.

She spun around and leaned against the counter. "I wanted to see what you'd do."

He narrowed his eyes. "I don't like games, Elsa. I'm too damned old for them."

"And I don't have time to wait for a man to decide if he likes me or not." She crossed her arms and glared at him. "Seriously, Trenton. I spent over a week waiting for you to call."

"I was busy."

"Too busy to call?" She was about to roll her eyes, but stopped midway and turned toward the sputtering coffee pot. "How do you take it?"

"With honesty and integrity." He knew she was referring to the coffee, but it seemed like the perfect opportunity to make his point.

"Don't talk to me about honesty and integrity. I've got that in abundance, but you ... they don't call you Mr. Van der Mean for nothing."

She picked up the cup and handed it to him, then

walked past him to the living room, where she sat in the corner chair. She looked like she belonged there, and he could see a fire burning in the fireplace, and Elsa sitting in that chair, blanket across her lap, with a copy of *Pride and Prejudice* in her hands.

He sipped his coffee, which burned all the way down, or maybe it was the bitterness of her words that stung.

"Who calls me that?"

She let her head hang and her shoulders sag. "My daughter."

"Being mean and being dishonest are two different things. Sure, I can be mean, but everyone can." He pointed toward the door. "You just kissed a man in front of me. Tell me that wasn't mean. I literally packed up my shit and moved to Aspen Cove for you. Imagine what I feel like when I see you kissing another man."

"You came here for me?"

He nodded. "Mostly for you." He knew he'd struck home when the light dimmed in her eyes.

"I'm sorry Trenton. I ... I obviously was having a moment, and I let my inner five-year-old take over. I didn't like that you didn't call me, especially after we shared that earth-moving kiss."

He smiled because he thought the same about their first kiss.

"Earth-moving, huh?"

She nodded. "At least a seven on the Richter scale."

He chuckled. "Only a seven? I'm going to have to up my game."

"Did you really pack up your sh ... stuff and move here?"

He couldn't believe it himself, but he did. "I have more here in Aspen Cove than I do in Denver. There's my son, and several properties that need re-furbing and you."

"Where are you going to live?"

If she liked games, he'd play a little one with her.

"Well, here, of course. I just assumed, since I gave you a good deal, that you'd happily let me stay. I take the right side of the bed."

She stared at him for a long moment. "You what?"

He grinned. "I sleep on the right side."

"You're not staying here. That wasn't part of the agreement."

His shoulders shook as his laughter took over. "We had an agreement?"

"Well, no, but normally the house purchaser doesn't have to supply a bed to the seller."

She was making this too easy. "Oh, honey, not just any bed. Your bed. It was in the fine print. Didn't you read it?"

She rose from her seat and went to a desk that sat

between the two front windows. In the drawer was the folder from the sale of the house. She picked it up and went straight to him, thrusting the documents in his direction.

"Show me."

He reached past the folder to grab her arm and pulled her into his lap. "How about we start over?"

She sat cradled in his arms, and it felt so perfectly right that he wasn't sure he'd ever let her go. He didn't know her well, but he'd known enough bad people to know that Elsa was all good.

She wiggled and moved on his lap until she was staring into his eyes.

"Hello," she said. "I'm Elsa Buchanan."

He cupped her cheeks and held her there. "I'm Trenton Van der Veen, not to be confused with my doppelganger, Trenton Van der Mean."

"Tell me about yourself, Trenton." She relaxed against him and placed her head on his shoulder.

"I'm a divorcee and the father of one boy named Mason. I'm the youngest of three and come from a long line of successful real estate moguls."

"Ooh, a mogul?"

"I'm more than my bank account."

She giggled like a schoolgirl. "I'm not after your bank account. Money is great, but I've never seen a U-Haul full of cash following a hearse to the burial site. Can't take it with you. In my opinion, you never need more than enough."

He kept his hand on her cheek. Her skin was velvet soft and as young looking as a woman in her thirties. Elsa may have been in her fifties, but she didn't look it. Men were at a disadvantage because women didn't seem to age these days. Fifty was the new thirty. An odd thought crossed his mind. He wanted to see what she'd look like at sixty and seventy and beyond.

"How do you know when you have enough?"

"I'd say you're there if you have to ask that question."

"I don't have enough." He was deadpan serious. "Of what?"

He pulled her closer and covered her mouth with his. He only pulled back long enough to say, "Of you," before he continued his assault on her mouth. Kissing Elsa was like seeing the sun after a biblical flood. After another minute of kissing her, he couldn't breathe. She literally took the air from his lungs.

"That was definitely an eight."

He shook his head. She would either bring him the life that he desired or be the death of him. Either way, he knew there wouldn't be a dull moment with the beautiful and intriguing Elsa Buchanan.

"Are you hungry?" He was starving.

"I just turned down a lunch date with Lloyd."

"Smart girl." He shifted her to her feet. "I don't like to share." Just the thought of her with someone else brought back terrible memories. "Unless it's a plate of onion rings."

She smoothed her hands over her jeans. "What about pie? What if I wanted a bite of your cherry pie?"

He let out a gasp. "My pie," he repeated while shaking his head. "I don't know. That's a lot to ask on a first date."

She held up two fingers. "Second. It's our second date."

He rose and stood in front of her. "You wanted to start over again, so that makes this our first."

She covered her mouth with her hand. "Oh my gosh, that makes me easy. I never kiss on the first date."

"I bet you would have kissed me."

She lifted her shoulders. "We'll never know because you left me on the doorstep." She fisted her hips. "You have a bad habit of leaving me, Trenton. I think you need to break that fast."

He reached forward and moved the strand of hair that had fallen across her cheek. "And you have a bad habit of..." He tried to think of something, only his mind drew a blank.

"Of what?"

He gave her a quick kiss on the lips. "Of distracting me." He stared into her eyes which he once thought looked like cornflowers but now looked like the blue from the boxes at Tiffany's.

Her stomach growled. "I only had a muffin," she said sheepishly.

"Then let's go to Maisey's. I'm sure she's got something to fill you up."

Elsa grabbed her purse from the entry table and followed him to his car. As usual, she waited until he opened her door. Some men would feel offended that she required old-fashioned manners, but it was a breath of fresh air for him. He was raised on old school values.

He believed that women were equal and if a woman wanted to open her own door, that was fine by him, too. He liked Elsa for many reasons, but one was because she was a fierce woman who lived by her set of rules. He had the impression that a man would never define who she was. If he was with Elsa Buchanan, it wasn't for any other reason than she wanted him there.

He opened the door and helped her inside before rounding the front to drive.

"Did you really think you were going to live with me?" She twisted in her seat to face him.

"Of course," he teased.

"You did not."

He chuckled. "You're right. I did not. I'm lucky enough to have Jewel on my side. She's given me use of the apartment above The Corner Store as long as I don't ransack the shelves in the middle of the night."

"That's no fun."

He pulled down the street and headed for Maisey's. "I agree, but given my Van der Mean reputation, I better stay on my best behavior."

They arrived on Main Street and he parked in front of Cove Cuts. Once they were both out of the car, he took her hand in his and walked to Maisey's. With a sweep of his hand, he opened the door and said, "After you."

Elsa took one step inside before he heard someone yell, "Be careful." He looked up to see Maisey running forward with a yellow caution sign, but it was too late for Elsa. She was already on the ground and clutching the arm that broke her fall.

She didn't make a sound, but tears sprang from her eyes.

"I got you," he said and bent over to sweep her up into his arms. One look at her wrist and he feared she'd broken it.

"Oh, my goodness," Maisey said. "I was just coming over to put this here sign down. We had a spill and ..." She shook her head. "I'm so sorry."

Elsa put on a brave smile. "It's okay," she said

with a shaky breath. She turned to look at him. "Put me down, Trenton. I didn't break my leg."

He didn't want to put her down, but did as she asked.

"Let's see Doc."

She frowned. "But I'm hungry."

Maisey pulled her pad from her pocket. "You see Doc and tell him to send me the bill and I'll get whatever you want started on the house."

Elsa ordered the chicken fried steak and mashed potatoes, and he ordered the blue plate special of meatloaf and mash.

As soon as Elsa winced again, he hurried her out the door and down to Doc's. When they walked inside, Agatha was behind the counter. He'd gotten all the details on the town when he'd been looking into his son.

"Morning, Agatha," he said.

She looked at him as if trying to place him. "Morning? Half the day is over."

To his memory, she sounded just like Doc, the old curmudgeonly man who'd been in Aspen Cove probably longer than the pines that grew there.

"Elsa has had a mishap in the diner and needs to be seen by Doc."

Agatha went to the stairs that led upstairs. "Hey love," she said sweetly. "You've got a live one."

Doc made it down the stairs slowly and when he

arrived, he looked at Trenton like he was a fly that needed to be swatted. His family's reputation in town had never been good. Probably because they bought up most of the surrounding land early on and sold it at a premium.

"Elsa has taken a fall at the diner, and I fear her wrist is broken."

Doc eyed him. "And when did you get your physician's license?" He shuffled toward the hallway. "Are you coming, or do you need a gurney?"

"Yep, the same old grumpy geezer."

"I'm coming," Elsa said and looked at Trenton. "What did you do to him?"

"Nothing," he said defensively. "It's just that my family has roots in this town."

"Weeds," Doc called back. "His family was a bunch of weeds amongst the flowers."

"Wow. Maybe you should stay out here. I don't want him taking his agitation at you out on me."

He shook his head. "No way. You fell on my watch, and there's no way I'm not coming in."

She smiled. "Is this your knight in shining armor act?"

He wrapped his arm around her shoulders and led her to the exam room.

"This is no act, sweetheart."

TWO HOURS later and Elsa was in a pink cast and hangry.

"I'm hungry," she said.

"And I'll feed you. Maisey brought our meals to go, but I asked her to take them back."

Elsa frowned. "Why did you do that?"

He walked her to the door to the diner. "Because I knew it would take some time, and I didn't want you to get food poisoning too."

"Aww, you care."

"I do."

They sat in a booth, and Maisey rushed out of the kitchen with fresh plates of hot food. "I'm so sorry. Please don't sue me." Her face was blanched of all color.

Elsa waved her cast-covered hand and grimaced. "I'm not suing you. What's the point?" She looked at Trenton. "I've got enough."

After a sigh of relief, Maisey left, and Elsa looked down at her plate. "I'm in trouble now." She did her best to use the silverware, but she couldn't grip the knife to cut through the meat.

He moved her plate toward him and cut her meal into bite-sized pieces.

"Looks like I'm moving in after all. You need me."

CHAPTER SEVEN

Sometimes Elsa wanted to bury her head in the sand. This was one of those times. She had prided herself on being independent. She never needed a man or, more accurately, she never wanted to have to count on one.

In her experience, the men who attracted her— the ones she chose—were often undependable. They never let her down in letting her down.

"You are not moving in with me." She stabbed at a piece of chicken fried steak. "Why do you think they call it chicken fried steak?"

He smiled at her. "It's because it's breaded and deep fried like chicken and don't change the subject."

She put a bite in her mouth and hummed her satisfaction. "Anything dipped in batter and deep fried should be against the law because it's criminally good." She wasn't ready to face the truth. She probably needed some help. Her right hand was in a cast, and that was her dominant hand. While many things could be ambidextrous tasks, she'd need her right hand to drive.

"Elsa, I'm not asking to ravage your body. I'm offering to help you while you're handicapped." He nodded toward her cast.

"A cast isn't a handicap, and why don't you want to ravage my body? What's wrong with it?" She knew she was being unreasonable, but she was tired and cranky, and she hated feeling helpless.

"Are you done?" He sat back and watched her for a moment.

"Done?" she asked. "Done with what?"

"With whatever is bringing this about." He swirled his hand in the air.

She let out an exasperated breath.

"Yes, I'm done." She looked at her plate and slowly lifted her head to meet his eyes. Trenton had been a godsend, and she was punishing him for being in the right place at the wrong time. "And I'm grateful for your help. I'm sorry I was being a crabby pants."

His lips lifted into a smile. "By the way, you look amazing in those pants."

A rush of heat coursed through her body. It was

either a hot flash or a response to his compliment. Both were possible.

"Thank you. They are just old jeans."

She watched his eyes darken like a cloudy storm was brewing behind them.

"Jeans that fit you like a glove. You—"

She held up her hand to stop him. "Don't say it."

He cocked his head to the side. "Say what?"

She pursed her lips for a split second. "That I look good for my age."

He chuckled. "You look good, no matter your age. I'm told that age is simply a number, and your youthfulness doesn't show in your reflection but in your heart."

A single butterfly whirled through her stomach and picked up friends until she was sure an entire kaleidoscope circled her belly.

"Who are you and where did you hide the Trenton Van der Veen everyone knows and loves ... to dislike?"

"I got a makeover. It's amazing what happens when you drop a hundred and twenty-eight pounds of dead weight."

"Was it that bad?"

"I don't divorce and tell, but it wasn't good. Now, it's in the past, and I'm trying hard to build a new future."

She forked a bite and chewed on it, along with

his words. She came to Aspen Cove to start over, but had she really? Her body was in Aspen Cove, but in her mind she was still the old girl from Denver.

"What does the future look like?"

She would be curious to see what picture of nirvana Trenton painted in his mind.

He scooped up a bite of mashed potatoes and gravy and seemed to savor the taste as it coated his tongue. It was the same look he had on his face after he kissed her.

A satisfied look glowed on his skin, and it made her skin tingle.

"I'm not exactly sure." He put his fork down and relaxed against the red bench. In the background the jukebox belted out a sixties tune called "Cry to Me," while Maisey danced around the tables, swinging a pot of coffee like it was her dance partner.

"Surely, you came here looking for something?"

"Yes, I came here looking for redemption."

"From whom?"

He rubbed his jawline. "The only one who can forgive me for my misdeeds is me, but I hope my presence will help me mend fences with Mason. He's his mother's son, or I thought he was until he walked away from everything for love."

"I read once that people are in your life at the time and in the right moment to teach you something about yourself or to learn a lesson you have to give. Who do you think taught who in your son's case?"

Trenton slid his half-eaten plate to the side. "My ego would like it to be me who taught him, but he taught me that power didn't come from possession. True power came from letting go. He was willing to ..." He shook his head. "Nope, he gave up everything for love. That's powerful. All my life I was taught that in the end, the man with the most toys wins. What good are toys if you can't play well with others?"

She moved the peas around her plate. "I was taught that the only thing you leave behind is memories. How do you want people to remember you?"

He chuckled. "Not as Mr. Van der Mean. What about you?"

She smiled. "I fear I'll always be the mother who punctured the Trojans."

"Looks like we've got some stuff to work on."

She nodded. "Do you want to help me go through the box Lloyd brought?"

He lifted a brow. "The gift?"

She took the last bite of chicken and moved her plate to the edge of the table.

"It wasn't a gift, per se. It's more of a project. Doc saddled me with organizing the town's historical documents. Lloyd had a box of things he thought I could use."

"And you kissed him for that." He grinned. "What if I said I had two boxes of historical documents?"

She wanted to laugh, but wasn't sure if he was teasing or serious.

"Do you?"

He shook his head. "No, but hypothetically, what would I get?"

Her insides were screaming "everything," but Trenton was a man who was used to getting what he wanted, and Elsa wouldn't be that easy. If, and when, he finally got her, if that's where this attraction was heading, then he'd have to work for it.

"A sock in the arm," she teased.

He looked shocked, then grabbed his arm and rubbed it. "Ouch. The cowboy gets a kiss and I get … nothing."

She reached across with her uninjured hand. "Not true. You got a good wallop which you'd feel longer than a kiss."

"Why not a kiss?"

She held his hand and squeezed it. "Because one box is fun but two is work." She slid from the booth. "Can you pay her? I'll pay you back when you take me home." She didn't say my home, which made her wonder if somewhere deep inside, she was considering his offer to stay.

"I always pay for my dates."

"Was this a date?" she asked.

He set several twenties on the table. "Every time I'm with you feels like a date."

Maisey rushed over and swiped the twenties off the table and tried to hand them back. "I told you I was buying."

Trenton curled his hand over hers, forcing her to take the bills back.

"No one is suing you. Besides, you have a grand-baby on the way."

Maisey raised on tiptoes and kissed his cheek. "I promise not to listen to all the bad things people say about you. You're okay in my book."

He turned to Elsa. "See?" He shrugged. "I've got a lot of ground to make up here."

Elsa walked ahead of him but looked over her shoulder. "You know what they say about biting off a lot?"

He shook his head. "You mean biting off more than I can chew?"

She laughed. "No, I mean, when you have a big task ahead of you, it's like eating an elephant. There's only one way to do that. One bite at a time."

He pressed his palm to the small of her back and led her outside, where they were accosted by Beth and Gray.

"Why didn't you tell me you fell and broke your arm?" Beth looked panicked.

"Because it happened so fast, and I needed medical attention." She looked up at Trenton. "Besides, Trenton was here."

Beth frowned. "Where that man is, bad follows."

"Beth," she warned. "He took me to Doc's and stayed with me."

"I would have done the same," Beth said.

Gray added. "All you have to do is call. We'll be right there."

Elsa touched her daughter's shoulder. "I was okay."

"You could have told me after."

Trenton cleared his throat. "Your mom was hangry."

Gray tried to suppress his laughter. "Say no more." He turned to Beth. "You know hangry."

She frowned. "Speaking of, I'm getting there now." She rubbed her stomach.

"And we're off," Gray said. "If you two need anything, just holler."

As they headed off, she heard Beth tell Gray, "Don't act like they're a couple. He's not my mother's type."

Trenton helped her into his car. When he rounded the front and took his place behind the wheel, he said, "You have a type?"

"Sure, everyone does."

"And?" He waited there with his hand on the ignition and his eyes on her.

"And she's right. You're not my type. I go for egotistical assholes."

He smiled. "Then I'm exactly your type."

She knew he was. She liked alpha men who knew their way around the world, but those types hadn't been all unicorns and rainbows for her.

"I'm trying something new."

He leaned into her personal space and placed a kiss on her lips before saying, "Me too. Let's see where this goes."

CHAPTER EIGHT

She took two painkillers and walked him to the door, wishing him a pleasant evening before closing and locking it.

God's gift to Trenton was difficult women. He sat in his car and looked at Elsa's front door, willing her to tell him to come back inside, but after five minutes of waiting, she didn't.

He put the car in reverse and headed toward The Corner Store and the efficiency apartment above it. He couldn't believe Philip and Marge, the previous owners, lived in the small space together for years. It was proof that Elsa was right. You only need enough, but he needed more.

He pulled into the alleyway parking and as he

got out of the car, Beth was closing. She stared at him and grumbled something under her breath.

"You can leave it open; I'm going up."

"She gave you a key?"

He pulled his ring from his pocket and jingled it in the air. "I'm all legal and everything."

"Don't mess up my inventory by snacking on the supplies."

He walked closer. "I know you don't like me, but I'll prove to you that I'm not who you think I am."

She stood taller. "And who do you think I think you are?"

She was talking in circles.

"Someone who will hurt your mother."

She stood with her lips parted as if the words she wanted to say were right there, but didn't have the momentum to escape.

"My mother is a stubborn pain in the ass, but she's a good human."

He nodded and grasped the door handle.

"She is all of those things."

She walked a few steps toward her car. "You know ... she may hurt you."

That was a real possibility.

"Thank you for the warning, but I'm not a quitter."

She laughed. "Now you sound like her. Maybe you are peas from the same pod." He watched her walk to her car, climb behind the wheel and back away.

He opened the door to the store and changed his mind. He wasn't ready to call it a night and hole up in a box with a full bed and little else.

He locked the store up and headed to Bishop's Brewhouse. He entered through the back door and wound through the narrow hallway to come out near the bar. There wasn't much going on in town, so the crowd was minimal. He recognized the Coopers who built prefab houses that went up like Lego kits. He had to admit that for homes built for sustainability, they were quite nice. In the corner were a couple of cowboy types, probably from Lloyd's ranch. It still irked him some that Lloyd Dawson had his lips on Elsa.

He had to redirect his thoughts and found Doc sitting at the bar stroking an orange cat that was missing an eye.

Doc patted the seat next to him. "Come and have a seat and you can buy me a beer."

"Oh, I can, can I?"

"It's my fee for advice."

Trenton walked over and took the stool to Doc's left.

"I'm not seeking advice."

Doc chuckled. "You just don't know it yet."

Cannon Bishop stopped in front of the two men. "What's it going to be?" he asked.

Trenton pointed to Doc's mostly-empty glass. "Whatever he's having times two."

Cannon pulled two frosted mugs from under the counter and pulled the taps. When the mugs were full, he slid them forward and disappeared into the back room.

"Those boys have turned out well." Trenton sipped his beer and thought about Mason. He'd turned out well, too. Had he ever told him how proud he was of him? A deep ache like a tear in his heart made him wince.

"They aren't without their problems. Everybody has got one or two."

"What about you?" He nodded to Doc. "What's your problem?"

Doc threw his hands in the air. "I work with all women. If that ain't hell, I'm not sure what is. Then again, there are days it's pure heaven. The problem is, you're never sure what you're walking into."

"Women can be a challenge."

Doc turned and looked at him. "How does it feel to be back?"

It was a lifetime ago that the Van der Veens lived in Aspen Cove. They were closely connected to all the major real estate in town. His father once said they were prospectors—miners of real estate. While others collected gold and silver nuggets, the Van der Veens collected acreage and enemies.

"It's been so long, but it seems like yesterday that I was running up the street trying to get my kite to catch a breeze."

Doc smiled. "Would that be the kite you made with sticks? The one that crashed through my front window?"

"Hey, I worked all summer paying that back."

"And ate your weight in candy. I'm not sure you didn't cost me more by working off the debt."

"You're probably right. I had a thing for Abba-Zabas."

"Couldn't keep enough of them stocked to fill your appetite."

"I haven't had one in years. I've quit the addiction."

"What brings you back?"

"I need to move forward with my life. I've spent it living on the corner of anger and regret. It was a busy intersection."

"I know what you mean. You can't get through life without regrets. Think of them as lessons learned. I've collected a lot of regrets over the years. The one thing I know is they serve no purpose in the future if you didn't learn from the mistakes of the past."

Trenton gulped his beer, trying to swallow what felt like a lump in his throat.

"How can you live a new future if people won't let you move out of the past?"

Doc took a drink of his beer and came out with a mustache covered in foam. He picked up a napkin riddled with x's and o's and wiped it clean.

"My pappy used to say that you can do ten good things, but if you do one bad thing, in people's minds, all the good is erased. Seems unfair."

"Damn right. So, what's the solution?"

"You can't care what people think, and if you do, then you stick it out long enough to prove them wrong. Eventually the good will outweigh the bad."

"I might not live long enough to see that happen."

"You going somewhere?" Doc wiped the condensation from the outside of his mug and folded the wet napkin.

"Not planning on it."

"We should live life one day at a time. It's all we're truly given. We can make plans for the future, but that's just a dream. The past is already gone. The future isn't here. All we have is the present, and that's exactly what it is, a gift."

Doc gave him advice all right. In a friendly way, Doc told him to be nice and to stick around long enough for people to notice.

"You're right. Live in the moment." He raised his glass to toast. "For all the moments we're blessed with." He tapped Doc's glass and drank deeply from his.

"Speaking of moments, why are you here with me when you could be with the lovely Elsa Buchanan?"

He looked into his beer. "She kicked me out."

"Not playing well with others yet?" Doc finished his beer and slid his mug to the edge of the bar. "It's like muscle memory. Do it enough and it comes naturally."

He shook his head. "No, she took a couple of pain relievers and I think she was heading to bed."

"She's got a lot on her plate. I'm sure she just needed space to think."

Doc was probably right. She'd just moved. She had two grandchildren on the way, and she broke her wrist. "Are you sure it's just a hairline fracture?"

"Are you questioning my abilities? Now listen here, son, I may be old, but I'm not done. I've got a few more good years in these bones. I'll be healing people until the day they bury me."

Trenton patted the old man on the back.

"Let's make sure that's a long time from now."

Doc slid off the stool. "I've got to be going. My Agatha likes to watch *Dancing with Stars*."

"Hey, Doc, I'm sorry about Phyllis. I always liked her."

"Because she was likable. I liked her too, son."
Doc put his hand on Trenton's shoulder. "Not
everyone comes into your life to stay forever. Love
them when they're here. Miss them when they're
gone. Never forget the lessons they taught you.
Phyllis was the embodiment of love. If we're lucky,
we sometimes get a second chance to fall in love all
over again." Doc turned and shuffled toward the
door. "What will you do with your second chance?"
he asked before he walked out the door.

That was the million-dollar question.

Cannon walked out of the back with a smile on
his face. "He left you with the bill, didn't he?"

He pulled the credit card from his wallet. "I'm
happy to pay it. Cheaper than a therapist."

Cannon nodded as he took the card. "Definitely,
but probably not as tactful. However, I'd say he can
deliver a message with a punch. What did you learn
today?"

Trenton pointed to his empty glass. "Can I have
another before you cash me out?"

Cannon fixed him up with another frosted
mug.

"That man is like a second father to everyone in
this town, so whatever he told you is probably God's
honest truth."

What was the message? There were so many, but
the ones that resonated the most were that he had to

overcome the bad with good and that after a failed marriage, there was hope for love.

"He told me to live in the present."

Cannon nodded his head. "That's a wise one. Did he also tell you if what you were facing was big, you needed to eat it like you'd eat an elephant? One bite at a time?"

"No, Elsa told me that."

"I'd say she's a wise woman."

"I'd agree."

Cannon rubbed the shadow along his jawline. "Hey, do you think elephant tastes like chicken?"

CHAPTER NINE

How was she supposed to drive herself to her doctor's appointment when she couldn't button her pants?

After a long, frustrated growl, Elsa shimmied out of her jeans and tossed them to the side, trading them and a T-shirt for a maxi-dress that didn't require fastening, zipping, or tying.

She'd never been a needy woman and didn't want to start now, but damn it – it looked like she would need help, whether she liked it or not.

There was no way she was calling Beth because she'd have to answer questions she didn't have answers for. Merrick would also be problematic because he was a cop and would dig until he got to the bottom of things.

With no one else to turn to, she picked up her phone and called Trenton.

"Good morning, Elsa," he said in a far too chipper mood. No man who woke up at seven happy should be trusted.

"Trenton?"

"Yes, Elsa. Are you okay?" There was a genuine tone of concern.

"Well..." She thought about his question. "I'm okay, but in a bit of a pickle."

"Oh, a pickle. That sounds worrisome."

She could imagine the light dancing in his eyes as his voice carried a hint of humor.

"Let me get to the point."

He chuckled. "That might be good."

"I need you." She shook her head. "What I mean is, I need your help."

"I'm halfway there."

"You're what?" She moved toward her door and saw his car racing down the street. "Oh, my goodness, you're already here."

She stepped out the door, still talking on the phone, but watching him walk toward her.

When he got to her, he said, "Do you want to hang up and talk in person, or should I stay on the line?"

She shot her arm out to wallop him but thought better of it. She was just getting used to the dull ache from the break and didn't want to exacerbate her problems.

She pulled her phone from her ear. "Why are you here?"

He cocked his head. "Because you called."

She turned and walked into the house, waving with her good hand for him to follow. "I know I called, but it's like you were already halfway here when I did."

He closed the door behind him. "No, but I heard something in your voice, and it told me you needed something."

She smiled. "Why doesn't that work when I have a hankering for Chinese food? Or a good tikka masala?"

"You won't find either of those in Aspen Cove."

He looked at her like she was a delicious plate of food.

"What?" She looked down to make sure the hem wasn't tucked in her panties. Not sexy panties like most youthful people wore, but her white cotton granny panties because they were comfortable. They might look like a diaper, but they felt like a cotton cloud supporting her bottom.

"You look beautiful."

A ribbon of warmth spread across her skin.

"This old thing?" She twirled in a circle. "I've had it for years."

He stepped forward and looked at her with heat in his eyes. "Classics never get old." He brushed aside a strand of hair that fell over her face. "When you called, I was worried."

She inhaled deeply. It was hard for her to ask for help. She'd been alone most of her life. The times she'd counted on a man to be there were times they tucked tail and ran.

"I couldn't button my pants."

His right brow lifted. "That is an emergency and while I can't say I'm a master at putting a woman's clothes on, in my day, I was pretty adept at removing them."

"Braggart."

"And the reason you need me now?"

There was a wistful longing in Trenton's eyes. She knew some of his story. Much like her, love had disillusioned him.

"I have an appointment of sorts in Copper Creek, and I don't know if it's wise to drive with a broken arm on the winding mountain road. I was hoping you might drive me."

He made a dramatic roll of his arm and bent at the waist.

"Your chariot awaits."

"I really appreciate it. If you'd be so kind as to stop by the bakery, I'd be happy to buy coffee and muffins."

He smiled so broadly she could see his back teeth.

"I was picking us up coffee and muffins before you called. In fact, I was already in the car."

"You didn't even know if I'd answer the door."

He chuckled. "That's why I brought bribes."

She narrowed her eyes but in a playful way. "What kind of bribes?"

He set his hand on the small of her back. He was always so gentle that if the heat of his palm wasn't there, she wouldn't feel his guidance.

As they walked back to the door, she took her bag and keys from the entry table and opened the door.

"I've got coffee with a splash of honesty and integrity."

That had been an exchange between them yesterday.

"Okay, what else?"

They moved toward the car, and she waited for him to open her door. Before, it was to set a precedent, but now it was because she was right-handed, and it felt odd to her to open the door with her left.

"Raspberry muffins." He opened her door and helped her inside. The interior smelled like Starbucks and a chocolate candy bar had a baby.

Trenton slid behind the steering wheel.

"And those brownies you love."

"We love," she corrected.

"I got several." He started the car and looked at her.

"What?" she asked.

"Where are we going?"

Her hand came to her mouth with a gasp and a giggle. "Right, directions would be good."

He shrugged. "Helpful, for sure."

She gave him the address, and they were off.

She sipped the coffee and considered the sweet gesture.

"Why anyone would consider you mean, I don't understand."

"It's well deserved."

She liked that he was willing to admit his shortcomings.

"I've been known to be mean too."

He glanced quickly in her direction. "That's expected. You were a librarian."

It felt odd to use the word "were" because being a librarian wasn't only what she did, but it was a genuine part of who she was.

"Books are in my blood. When I have lab tests, they don't say you have healthy O positive. They look perplexed and say you have healthy A to Z positive."

"Well, as long as you're healthy. No one has time to be sick. There's too much living to do to die now."

Her heart hammered until she was certain the ache inside her chest was from bruising.

"Yes, it's always the goal to stay healthy."

He picked up his cup and took a sip and then placed it back into the holder.

"Why are you going to the doctor? Can't Doc Parker see you?"

She stared out the window. It was spring, and the aspens that the cove was named after were getting their leaves. Soon they would be big enough to quake in the wind and the sound of rustling would fill the air.

"I saw him. This is ..." What did she tell him? If she wasn't sharing this with her daughter and son, she wouldn't tell Trenton. Besides, she liked him too much to lose him already. No man wanted to be saddled with a girlfriend who was sick. Right now, there was nothing to share.

"It's a girl thing."

He held up his hand. "Got it."

Happy to have that part of their conversation over, she reached into the bag and pulled out two brownies. After wrapping one in a napkin and handing it to him, she took a bite of hers. A hum of satisfaction left her lips.

"Oh my, that is so good." She took another nibble. "I've had at least a dozen of these, and each time, it's like I'm having it for the first time. It's almost as good as sex." She nearly choked on her brownie when she realized what she had said.

He glanced at her before turning his focus back to the road.

"The brownies are good, but not that good. If you're comparing sex to brownies, then I imagine you haven't had a man truly make love to you."

In all her years, that was probably true. The words of love slipped from their lips easily enough, but that was probably to get to the as-delicious-as-a-brownie part.

"Do you think there's a difference between making love and having sex?"

He didn't waste any time to answer. "Yes. A world of difference. If it's just sex, then only your body is involved. But, when you make love, your heart is involved, and that makes all the difference."

What he said made sense. With the men she shared intimacy with, there was love—on her part.

"How many women have you said 'I love you' to, just to get in their knickers?"

"None." He was so adamant.

"Never?"

"I've only ever told one woman that I loved her and that was Priscilla."

"You didn't tell your lovers?"

He shook his head. "I've always been honest, and sometimes that comes across as mean. From someone who had their heart ripped out and trampled on, I never mess with those three words."

"What do you mean, mess with them?" They were almost to Copper Creek.

He took in a deep breath. "It means that I will never utter those words unless I mean them. And the woman I say them to will be worthy of my love." He pulled into the parking lot of the medical center. "When I love ... I love hard. When I say those words, I mean forever. And if someone says them to me ... it's a promise."

She loved that whole concept, but forever and promises and love were as elusive as a four-leaf clover or a lottery win. The only love she'd ever known was the love of and for her children.

She reached for his hand and squeezed it. "You deserve love."

He nodded to the door. "Do you want me to come in with you or wait here?"

"Wait, please."

Not waiting for him to open her door, she un-buckled her seatbelt and reached awkwardly with her left hand to pull the handle.

"Let me help you."

"I got it." She pushed the door open, but he was there before she could swing her legs out.

"Elsa, let me help you." He held out his hand. "Please, let me be useful."

She put her hand in his, and he pulled her to her feet.

"Thank you, Trenton." She stared into his eyes. "I do need you."

He leaned down and brushed his lips against hers. "I need you, too."

ELSA LIKED DR. TRENDLE. As soon as she felt the lump in her breast, she set up a biopsy appointment. Luck was on her side because there was a cancellation, and she could have a core needle biopsy right then.

As they removed the tissue, Elsa explained how she'd been asking for months for someone to take her seriously.

"Never let anyone dismiss you. I always tell my patients to listen to their bodies, and yours is telling you something isn't right."

Elsa shivered. "I'm afraid that I might be right."

Dr. Trendle patted her shoulder. "It's nothing to worry about until we find out it's something to worry about. Let's get the results." She put the sample in a medical sleeve. "I've labeled this STAT."

"When will you know?"

"I'll call you as soon as I do."

As soon as she was bandaged and dressed, she left the clinic and found Trenton in his car with a grin on his face. He jumped out when he saw her.

"Are you okay?"

Her breast would be sore later, but she was good for now.

"Yes, I'm fine."

He narrowed his eyes.

"The one thing I know is when a woman says she's 'fine,' she's usually everything but. However, I have something that will make you more than fine." He opened the door and what greeted her was the scent of food. She wasn't sure what it was because it seemed to be a mixture of everything she loved.

"What did you do?"

He held up his phone. "I ordered delivery."

"You ordered food delivered to your car?"

He smiled. "I wasn't leaving you here."

She laughed. "You're a crazy man."

He helped her inside. "Maybe I'm just crazy for you."

"Be careful, I drive people crazy in a very different way."

"I'll take my chances."

She smiled. "I like a risk taker." She lifted her nose into the air and inhaled. "What did you get?"

CHAPTER TEN

Sitting in the driver's seat, he turned to her. "I got Chinese and Indian."

She bounced, smiling and clapping her hands. "It's a feast day."

Putting a smile on Elsa's face by buying food she liked was one of life's great joys. It had been a long time since bringing happiness to someone could be that cheap and easy. Not to say that Elsa was cheap or easy. She was complicated, and yet simple, fierce, and somehow sweet at the same time.

What mattered to his ex-wife didn't seem to take space in Elsa's life. Sure, she enjoyed nice things. That was clear by her book collection, and the pricey but comfortable furniture in her home. But money didn't define Elsa. She seemed to take great joy in simple stuff, like sharing a brownie sundae or a slice of pie. Reading a good book on a rainy day or watching a rerun of a classic movie.

"Do you want to stop somewhere and eat it or take it to your place?"

She glanced in the back at all the bags sitting in a row on the seat. "How much did you get?"

He lifted his shoulders. "More than I should have, but I wanted to make sure I got your favorites."

She shifted and winced when the seatbelt pulled against her breast.

"I like everything."

He chuckled. "I got everything."

After another look in the backseat, she faced forward.

"Let's go to my place. We can have Chinese for lunch and Indian for dinner."

"Are you asking me on a date?"

She waved him off. "Of course not; that would be forward of me."

He put his car in reverse and backed out of his parking spot, pulling onto the main road and heading toward Aspen Cove.

"You? Forward? I wouldn't think of it," he teased.

She settled her hands on her thighs. "If I were to ask you on a date, would you say yes?"

He wanted to pull the car over and kiss her again. "I'm not easy."

She looked out the window. "No, but if you bring your own food, then you're cheap."

He reached over to take her hand. "For you, I'll be anything." He let a moment pass so she could soak up his words. Elsa had put some kind of spell on him. Or maybe it was that he'd let go of the baggage of his past and the lightness it brought made him consider all the possibilities of a future.

"Tell you what," he said. "I think we should plate up our food and watch a classic."

"I only have a TV in my bedroom. I watch little television."

Inside, he was smiling. He definitely wanted to get into Elsa's bed, but never thought it would be over a plate of beef with broccoli.

"Mattress picnic it is."

She did this thing with her lips when she thought. She puckered them and moved them from side to side. He'd seen her do it several times. He'd call it her debating face or her consideration expression. Right now, he knew she was deciding whether to let him into her room—her bed. It wasn't a romantic gesture, but a familiar one. To let someone into your personal space, a room as intimate as a bedroom, meant something.

"You can't spill on my sheets."

He let out a faux gasp. "I'd never."

"What about *My Fair Lady*?"

That took him by surprise. He fully expected *Pride and Prejudice* or *Little Women.*

"No Mr. Darcy?"

"Who needs Darcy when I have Van der Veen?"

"Who indeed."

"GRAB EXTRA NAPKINS, WILL YOU?" Elsa called from the bedroom.

He picked up a stack from the counter and headed back to her room.

She'd pulled back her comforter and blanket to expose only the sheets. After piling up several pillows, she took the right side of the bed and he walked around to the left side.

"Did you find the movie?"

She nodded and lifted the remote. "Cable is amazing these days. You can find just about everything." She pressed play and *My Fair Lady* started. The movie was designed for theaters with a musical intro. If he remembered correctly, there was an intermission, which would be the perfect time to kiss Elsa. He had it all planned out. Dinner ... movie ... kiss.

"How many times have you watched this movie?"

She looked up and cocked her head right and left as if counting.

"Dozens of times. It's a yearly requirement, like *The Ten Commandments* or *Wizard of Oz* or *Ben Hur*. They're like M&Ms. You can't just have one."

"But the books are better, right?"

Her hand went to her heart. "Always, but there's something entertaining about the movies and how they are interpreted from the words."

He leaned back on the pillows and took in the tiny screen she had sitting on her dresser. It wasn't much bigger than a laptop. He wanted to laugh because the one at his home in Cherry Creek was the size of the wall. The funny thing was, he didn't enjoy it any more than he did this one. He realized that it wasn't what you had that mattered, but who you spent your time with that did.

"Colin Firth or Laurence Olivier?"

She looked at him like he had three heads.

"Mr. Higgins is Rex Harrison."

He chuckled.

"No, I meant for Darcy."

"Oh," she said and took a bite of moo goo gai pan. "While I love the classics and should choose Olivier, word has it he hated the part, and it shows. Hands down, Colin Firth."

"I agree. He makes a magical Darcy."

They sat and watched as Mr. Higgins turned a pauper into a princess while gorging on everything

Twin Dragons offered. During the intermission, he cleaned up the kitchen and put the food away.

As he returned to the bedroom to finish the movie, her phone rang.

He wasn't one to eavesdrop, but there wasn't a place in her house where he couldn't hear her side of the call. To give her some sense of privacy, he stood out of sight in the hallway. Words like, "okay," and "what's next?" sounded benign, but when she mentioned "surgery," his heart jumped a beat. There was another five minutes of talk before she hung up. He waited an additional minute before he entered to find her staring into space, her face as white as the rice they'd devoured.

He could play this two ways: he could pretend he heard nothing or he could come out and ask her directly. He opted for number one. Elsa was a private woman. He still hadn't gotten her to share the story of how she'd impregnated her two kids.

He walked into the room carrying two fortune cookies. With his two hands outstretched, he smiled.

"Pick a hand."

"What?" She shook her head.

"Fortune cookies. Pick a hand."

"Okay."

She pointed to his right, and he handed her the cookie.

"Eat the cookie first or the fortune doesn't come true," he said.

"Who told you that?"

He walked around the bed and took his place next to her, only this time he scooted in closer, so their bodies touched.

"It's common knowledge."

"If I've never heard it, it's not common knowledge."

"Just eat the cookie."

She broke it in half, careful to remove the paper fortune, and took a bite. With her mouth full, she said, "No one eats them because they taste like sawdust." She seemed to struggle to swallow but got the first half down.

"Are you an expert at eating sawdust?"

"No, but after lunch I'm an expert in eating Chinese."

"Finish it up; I want to see what yours says."

She looked at the cookie and frowned. "You first."

He broke his cookie and took out the fortune. Obviously, there was no accounting for taste because he liked fortune cookies and gobbled his down.

He straightened the slip of paper that held his fortune and read it aloud.

"Flattery will go far tonight."

She eyed him with skepticism. "You think?"

He leaned over and brushed her lips with his.

"You already let me in your bed."

She laughed, but it didn't reach her eyes. She was going through the motions of enjoying their time together, but he could sense that the call was bothering her.

"It's your turn."

He grabbed her remaining half of cookie. "I'll take one for the team." He popped it into his mouth and chewed.

"Your reality check is about to bounce." She stared at the fortune cookie for a moment. "Can we trade?" she said, handing hers to him.

"I don't think so." He looked down at her fortune and back at her blank expression. "You want to talk about the call?"

CHAPTER ELEVEN

"No, I don't." She wasn't about to blurt out that she had cancer. Talk about a downer for the evening. Even though she didn't want to share, she hated keeping it all bottled inside.

"Come on, Elsa. I know something is wrong. Just tell me."

She shook her head. "I'm not ready to share, yet."

He let out a huff. "You're great at clamming up. You drop crumbs of a story and then sweep them under the carpet. That's not fair."

"Lots of things aren't fair, like me getting breast cancer." She didn't mean to say that out loud, but it was out, and it hung in the air like a dark cloud.

"Oh, geez." He reached for her, but she pulled away.

"I don't want your pity." She hated feeling weak, and though she expected the diagnosis—knew it in her gut before they even took the biopsy—she wasn't prepared to hear the C word.

"I'm not offering you pity. I'm offering you strength."

She climbed off the bed and moved to the living room. "I've gotten through my life so far without a man. I don't need one now."

He moved down the hallway after her. "I get that you're a strong woman. You just received some jarring news. Let me hold you. I want to be here for you."

She moved in a circle as if she'd lost her bearings. She had no idea what to do with all the rage building inside her. Life wasn't fair. She'd just moved to a house she could enjoy for the rest of her life and now that life might not be as long as she expected. How long would she have to spend with her children and her grandchildren? Would they be years of joy or years consumed by illness? Then there was Trenton, a man whom she saw a future with but who wanted a lame horse? Sure, he was being supportive now, but what if she had to have chemo and lost her hair? What would happen when they took her breasts? He didn't sign up for that when he bought out the Chinese and Indian restaurants.

"You should go."

His eyes widened, and the blue of them turned murky.

"No, I'm not leaving you alone."

She stomped her foot, but it only made a hollow thud since she was barefooted.

"I'm not asking you. I'm telling you. I need you to leave."

He placed his hands on her shoulders. "Come on, Elsa. I know men have let you down in the past, but I'm not them." He yanked her to his chest.

She crashed against him and felt the warmth of his body and the strength of his embrace. She wanted him to stay, but needed him to go.

"Please," she cried against his shirt. "I can't do this in front of you."

He gripped her shoulders and stepped back just enough so he could see her.

"It's okay to be vulnerable. It's okay for you to let it go. I'm strong enough for both of us."

She'd never cried in front of any man, and she didn't want to start now, but the tears rushed down her cheeks. Embarrassment flooded her veins as she let out a sound that sounded more wounded animal than human.

He pulled her to him once more and held her so tightly it was hard to breathe, but she didn't leave his embrace. She rarely allowed herself a moment, but today, she'd let him hold her and console her. Today she'd be weak, because from this point on, she'd need to be strong.

Trenton didn't say a word. He hugged her and kissed the top of her head while she let years of anguish unfold. She cried about everything that had gone wrong in her life. If she was allowing herself this single breakdown, it had to count.

He shifted, moving a hand from her back to swoop her up behind her knees. He held her next to his chest as he walked with her to the corner chair and took a seat. She sat in his lap like a child and wept until her tears ran dry.

She pulled up her shirt and dried her cheeks. "I'm okay now."

He didn't let go. "If you don't mind, I'd like to hold you a while longer."

He relaxed his arms. She had the choice to stay or go, and she appreciated that. So many men asserted their power. In a way, Trenton had when he refused to leave. For that, she was grateful because while the burden of cancer hung over her head, she felt like she'd released a thousand-pound weight from her soul. Internal baggage weighed so damn much.

"I knew it. A couple months ago I found a lump, and I knew it, but my doctor dismissed me."

"You want me to have him investigated?"

"No, he's retiring soon. I'm sure he was pacifying

me until he left, and I could be someone else's problem."

Trenton rubbed her back. "You're never a problem, Elsa. His job was to listen to you. You should have used your librarian's voice."

She laughed. "That would have given the poor man a heart attack." She leaned her head on his shoulder. "You know, you didn't sign up for this holding and cajoling stuff. Hell, I don't even know if you're still signed up for anything."

He patted her leg. "I'm not going anywhere."

She set her hand on his chest. "Thank you for being stubborn and staying."

"Talk about stubborn. You need to let someone else bear the weight from time to time."

"No one has ever wanted to." She wondered if that was the truth or if she was too afraid to relinquish any control. The thing about making all the decisions in her life was that she only had herself to blame for the outcomes. Getting cancer wasn't something she could control, and that was what scared her the most.

"I'm here. Tell me what you need."

She rubbed her hand across his shirt. "This—this is exactly what I need."

He kissed her cheek. "This I can do."

For the next thirty minutes, they sat like that. Her in his lap and him saying nothing but saying everything by his presence. She thought about Trenton and his ex-wife. He said he wasn't a quitter, and neither was she. He refused to end a horrible marriage for fear of losing himself and she refused to enter one for fear of losing control.

"Nothing like a health predicament to show me I had no control all along."

He sighed. "Not true. You have control over your perspective. You don't have control over this situation, but you get to decide how you respond to it."

She soaked in his words for a minute. "I will beat this thing."

"Of that, I have no doubt."

"You want to finish *My Fair Lady*?"

"Will it make you feel better?"

She shrugged. "Probably not, but it gets us both in bed again."

He chuckled. "See, my fortune is coming true."

She sat back and punched him lightly in the arm. "Where's the flattery?"

He cupped her cheeks and pressed his forehead to hers.

"Elsa Buchanan, you are as frustrating as you are intriguing. You are beautiful and funny and have excellent taste in literature and food."

"Will you still like me when I don't have boobs?"

He smiled. "Can't miss something I haven't seen. Who needs boobs anyway?"

She slid off his lap. "Cows if we want milk to go with our brownies."

His brows lifted. "You've got brownies?"

She waved for him to follow her. "And milk."

"A woman after my heart."

"How did you know?" She turned around and lifted on tiptoes to kiss him, but didn't look to see his expression. Trenton thought he was there for the long haul, but as soon as he saw what he was up against, he'd be gone. That's how all the men in her life were. When the going got tough, the men got going. But for now, there were brownies and milk and Eliza Doolittle waiting.

"Do you think she likes who she's turned out to be?" she asked as the movie neared the end. "He changed her."

"Did he?" He fluffed his pillow and turned on his side to face her. "Can anyone truly change a person?"

She shimmied down the bed so she was next to him and staring into his soulful eyes.

"Are you saying that a leopard never changes its spots?" she asked.

He rubbed his chin, which now had a day's growth of whiskers. They were salt and pepper, like his hair.

"No, I'm saying that inside we never truly change. We will always internally respond in the way that is natural for us. But as we mature, we learn to run our thoughts through a system of checks and balances, and then we can respond in an adult way. It's never good to let your inner child speak for your adult self."

"So, when I told you I had cancer, what was your initial response?"

His lip twitched. She'd seen that happen several times over the course of their budding friendship. It always happened when he was divulging something about himself. It was almost like a lie detector, but this was a truth detector. Trenton didn't lie.

"Honestly, it scared the hell out of me."

"That's two of us." She scooted toward him and laid her head on his chest. It felt natural to be here in his arms. "You know, I don't expect you to see me through this." If he was being honest, then she could too. "It's a lot for anyone and we're just getting to know each other."

He set his hand on her hip and squeezed it. "I've kissed you. If you think I'm giving up more of those, you're crazy."

"You like my kisses?"

He nipped at her lower lip. "I'm crazy about your kisses."

She shifted, so they were chest to chest. "You're just crazy."

His mouth covered hers, and the kiss left her breathless. How could one kiss feel so good and say so much? It was like strength left his lips and entered her being. He was telling her she could trust him. She gripped him as if he'd disappear.

She pulled away and breathlessly asked, "Stay with me?"

CHAPTER TWELVE

Last night was the most innocent of all the nights he'd had with a woman who let him sleep in her bed, and yet, it was the best of his life.

"What's it going to be?" Maisey asked.

He sat at the counter and looked at the menu, which was silly because he knew what he'd order before he arrived.

"Two orders of cakes and eggs and two sides of bacon. Make it crisp, please."

Maisey wrote his order and walked away.

"Big appetite?" the guy next to him asked.

He looked familiar, but Trenton couldn't place the face.

"Buying for two," Trenton answered.

"Yeah, I heard you were back."

With a tilt of his head, Trenton turned so he could get a better look at the man. The brown eyes were common, but the mole on his chin was familiar. All the Ardens had them.

"Frank?"

The man chuckled.

"I was wondering when you'd figure it out." He offered his hand to shake. "Long time, no see."

Coming back to town was turning into a walk down memory lane.

"Do you still live here?"

Frank's head bobbed up and down and back and forth and Trenton couldn't decipher his answer.

"I still have the house on the lake."

It was a sweet piece of land. Any property on the water was hard to find and easy to sell. Trenton would do just about anything for that lake house. He wondered if Elsa would want to live on the water.

"Are you looking for a buyer?"

Frank definitively shook his head.

"No way. That house is a family legacy. I'm here occasionally, but I spend most of my time in Silver Springs. I've got an apartment and a law firm there."

"Another Aspen Cove boy who done good." It didn't surprise him; the Ardens were an intelligent group. "What happened to your sister?" Trenton smiled at the memory of Sara. She was his first kiss. They had dived off the cliff above the falls and hid under the veil of water where they made out like teens, but they were only eleven.

"Sara is a veterinarian and lives in Tulsa. She married and divorced. She's got a girl named Reese."

"Wow." It shouldn't surprise him because he'd married and divorced and had a son. It was funny how when you didn't see a person for a long time, they seemed to stay the same age. Sara would always be the person who'd taught him girls were a lot more fun if you played nice with them. Even more fun if you were a good kisser.

"I know. Time flies. My niece is coming to town for a bit. She plans to hole up in the house and write her blockbuster."

"Scriptwriter?"

He shook his head.

"Novelist."

"Wow. Is she any good?"

He shrugged. "I don't read romance, so I have no idea."

Maisey pushed through the swinging doors with a to-go bag in her hands.

"I put extra syrup and butter in there. Tell Elsa I said hello." She winked at him and walked away.

"Elsa?"

Trenton blushed. It wasn't a normal reaction for him, but each time he thought about her, he warmed inside.

"She's …" How did he describe her? They hadn't defined their relationship, but they were in one, even if she didn't know it. They'd kissed and slept together. It wasn't the usual way he ended up in a woman's bed. Generally, there was an expensive dinner, a glass or two of wine and some negligee. He slept in his clothes and Elsa changed into a flannel nightgown. He'd never seen anything so grandmotherly look so damn sexy on a woman. "She's new in town. A librarian by trade. Her daughter lives here."

Frank smiled. "Oh, the one who poked holes in her kids' condoms."

Trenton's eyes widened. "She what?"

Frank picked up his coffee mug. "It's a small town. You know how gossip spreads."

How could he forget?

"She's an amazing woman."

"She's something." Frank's lips curved into a smile. "Make sure you hide your condoms."

"It's not like that." He wanted it to be like that, but Elsa was facing a life-altering illness and her focus needed to be on getting healthy, not getting hooked up.

"I thought you were married?" Frank asked.

He was wondering how long it would take for his life to be the next round of gossip.

"I was, but it didn't work out." That wasn't quite

true. "It worked out for thirty years, but it was never right. Sometimes you marry the wrong girl for the right reasons. Sometimes you marry the right girl for the wrong reasons. Sometimes it's just plain bad all around."

Frank sipped his coffee while Trenton gathered extra napkins and checked the bag to make sure everything was there.

"Which was it for you?"

"At different points in the relationship, it was all of those things. What about you?"

"Confirmed bachelor. I'm married to the job."

With the bag in his hand, he looked at Frank.

"Jobs don't warm your heart or your bed."

Frank laughed. "They don't take half of everything when they're gone, either."

"That's true." It was funny to look back and see how much time he spent hanging on to things that didn't truly matter. If he drilled down, the only thing that mattered was people and he had been a poor example as a father and a friend and even a husband. He would do better. "I need to get this to Elsa before she wakes."

Frank waved. "Don't be a stranger."

Trenton stepped outside and made his way to his car, but before he could get in and close the door, Beth ran out of The Corner Store.

"You didn't come home last night."

He wanted to laugh, but he'd learned long ago that pregnant women were unpredictable.

"I wasn't aware that I have to check in with you."

She moved toward him like a raging bull—a bull wearing her hair in a bun.

"If you hurt my mother, I swear ..."

"Don't worry. I'm not going to hurt your mother. I thought we went through this."

She growled deep in her throat. He could tell that Beth would be a formidable mother. That growl alone would send her child into hiding.

"That was before you slept with her."

"I didn't sleep with your mother." He did, but not in the way she thought.

"Who did you sleep with if you didn't come home?"

"Look, I don't kiss and tell. If you want to know anything about me and your mother, ask her." He knew the two of them had to talk anyway and anything he said to defend her mother's honor or his could divulge information that Elsa wasn't ready to share. "Call your mother."

He waited for her to step back, and he closed the door. He'd taken far too much time picking up breakfast, and hoped Elsa was still asleep when he came back. He opened the door and smelled the coffee.

Sitting in the corner chair with her blanket

pulled to her neck was Elsa. She scrambled to wipe away the tears streaming down her face.

He rushed to her side and kneeled before her.

"What's wrong, love?"

She lifted her chin in what some would consider a haughty way, but he knew she was shoring up her strength.

She opened her mouth, and a squeak escaped. After clearing her throat several times, she dropped the blanket and sat up.

"I thought you'd left."

He pulled her to her feet and led her to the table.

"If I ever leave you, it's because you need something." He lifted the bag. "I got breakfast."

She smiled. "Bacon?"

He pulled out her chair so she could sit and then took out the containers of food.

"Yes, and pancakes and eggs, extra butter and syrup. Is there anything else you need?"

She nodded. "I need you."

"I'm here, and I'm not going anywhere."

She took a bite of bacon. The straightness in her spine softened.

"I love bacon."

He took his seat beside her. "Someday maybe you'll love me as much as you love cured pork." It wasn't something he intended to say out loud. Many people would consider him a fool for jumping into a relationship right after getting out of one. But his marriage had been over for decades, so in truth, he'd been single for most of it.

"Remember when you said you were going to move in here to help because of the cast?" She held up her broken wrist.

He nodded. "Yes."

She lowered her head. "I don't need you for that."

His heart sank. "That saddens me to hear that."

She reached for his hand and gripped it in hers.

"I didn't say I didn't need you. I just don't need you for that, but I need you for everything else. Are you willing to be my everything man for a while?"

Just then, he realized what it might feel like to be a woman who was waiting for her man to propose. This wasn't the same thing at all. He heard the words 'for a while,' which meant she expected an end to her need, but for now, he'd make her realize that letting him go would be her biggest mistake.

Elsa's phone rang and she reached for it.

"It's Beth."

He held up his hand, trying to signal to her to not take the call yet. He had things to tell her pertaining to Beth, but he didn't get a chance.

"Hello, darling."

Elsa held the phone away from her ear as Beth spewed out whatever she needed to get out. From his place nearby, it didn't seem like the woman took a breath.

Elsa frowned at him.

"What did he tell you?"

He mimed everything he could think of that said "nothing," from a wave of his hands to the zero he made with his fingers. All the while he shook his head. Elsa was a private woman. He was certain he wouldn't know she had cancer if he hadn't been there when the call came in.

"You don't get to judge me when you had a one-night stand with Gray that knocked you up."

Trenton leaned back and watched and listened to Elsa's side of the conversation.

"Yes, I know you had help, and I don't regret it. If I waited for the two of you to get your stuff together, I'd have a walker by the time my grandbabies were born. As it is, I'm already sprouting gray hair." She frowned and pointed to the phone before mouthing the words, "What did you say?"

"Nothing. I said nothing."

She narrowed her eyes as if she didn't believe him.

After a few minutes of Beth's nonstop chatter, Elsa smiled. He could tell she was up to something.

"Honey, I really need to go. Trenton brought extra syrup that I plan to drizzle over his body and lick it clean."

He heard a gasp come from the other end, followed by words he couldn't hear clearly.

"If you don't want to know about my life, then stop interrogating me. You don't need to hone those skills just yet. You've got a few years before your little one sneaks out the windows at night."

There was another rapid-fire response.

"Oh, yes, you did. Don't forget, I had to pick you up at the police station because you were out past curfew. Have a lovely day, sweetheart." Elsa hung up the phone.

"At what point do we become the children?" he asked.

"I should have never..." She stopped mid-sentence as if she caught herself before divulging her truth.

"Poked holes in their condoms?"

She sucked in a breath.

"How did you know?"

He chuckled. "It's a small town and gossip spreads like wildfire."

She huffed and crossed her arms. "People shouldn't tell tales."

"If they didn't, you would have been out of a job. Some of the best stories were handed down from person to person."

She didn't have a comeback, which was surprising because Elsa always seemed to have one. Instead, she poured a plastic cup of syrup on her now-cold pancakes.

"Thank you for breakfast."

He smiled and picked up a full container of syrup. "What's this about syrup and my body?"

CHAPTER THIRTEEN

"Too much sugar is bad for you." She forked a bite of maple-covered pancake and popped it into her mouth.

"It's okay to indulge a sweet tooth occasionally."

She loved the way he smiled. It was the kind that reached his beautiful blue eyes and made them sparkle like sapphires in the sun.

"I've got cancer. I don't want to add a major case of diabetes to it."

When she woke alone that morning, she figured her life would continue status quo. She'd have to deal with the ups and downs on her own. Trenton had told her he wouldn't leave, but he had. She never considered he'd gone out for breakfast. The man was a surprise at every turn. He wasn't who everyone thought he was. Then again, few people let their true selves out. Trenton was a tycoon and that came with a reputation of destruction and debauchery. She was a librarian and people thought of her as uptight and stuffy. Neither was what society had painted them to be.

He smirked at her.

"How about a minor case?"

She couldn't help but laugh.

"You'll have to work hard to get in my pants."

He shifted in his seat and tugged her from her chair into his lap.

"Oh, I don't want in your pants, but this granny gown ..." He whistled. "Now this is another story." He kissed her quickly and licked his lips like he was savoring the taste. She probably had syrup on hers.

"Sexy, right?"

He nodded. "Totally turns me on."

He was kidding, and she knew it, but she liked how playful he could be.

She ran her hands over the red plaid. "I've got one in blue plaid too."

His hands fell to her waist. "Only bring out the blue one if you're serious. That's my color."

"Oh, you have a color?"

He nipped at her lip. "Not just any color, it's got to be blue plaid."

"I'll keep that in mind."

All talking stopped when he kissed her again. It was the same kiss that he gave her yesterday. The kind that would catch a girl's clothes on fire.

Just as her hands came up to unbutton the top of her nightgown, the doorbell rang.

She jumped from his lap and raced toward the room.

"Can you get that?"

"What if it's one of your kids?" he called from the table.

"Say hi and let them in. No one sees me in my pajamas. Not even them."

"I've seen you."

She peeked out her bedroom door. "But you haven't seen the blue."

She watched him walk toward the door.

"A man can dream."

She quickly dressed in a pair of jeans and a button-down shirt. She stepped into her flats and pulled her hair into a ponytail as she stepped out of her room.

Standing in the living room was Doc Parker. In his hand was a large box.

"I brought over the archives. Thought you could get started."

Trenton took the box from Doc's arms.

"The archives are a single box? I thought you wanted a museum of sorts for the town," Elsa said.

Doc's bushy brows rose.

"I've got five more in my truck and a storage shed of interesting artifacts. Charlie has been wanting me to clean that out since she got here. She wants the space so her husband Trig can have a he shed."

"A he shed?" Trenton asked.

Doc shifted his lips so his mustache moved. It looked like a live animal gripping his upper lip. "Normally it's a she shed, but Charlie has claimed the entire house so she thought it might be nice for Trig to have a place he could call his own."

"I need a he shed," Trenton said.

Doc looked at her and then at Trenton.

"I thought you were staying above the market."

"I am. I was just—"

"He's not. He's staying with me. I'm going to need some extra help in the weeks to come and asked him to move in."

Doc frowned. "I don't know why all you youngsters are so keen to shack up. Back in my day, you bought the cow before you could milk it."

Elsa felt the heat rise to her cheeks. She wasn't sure if she should be mad or embarrassed and decided it was okay to be both.

"I am not shacking up with Trenton." She thought about Doc's words and his current situation. She knew he and Agatha were a couple, but didn't recall them being married. "Aren't you shacking up with Agatha?"

Doc grumbled something about *doing as I say and not as I do.*

"Make yourself useful, son, and grab those other boxes."

Trenton did as he was told and left to retrieve the boxes.

Doc walked into her kitchen and opened the cupboards until he found a mug, then poured himself a cup of coffee.

He lifted his steamy mug. "Do you mind?"

His coffee was already poured, and he was heading to her kitchen table.

"No, help yourself."

He looked around the house. "I like what you've done with the place. This house belonged to my Uncle Harvey."

That was interesting news. "What happened to him?" she asked.

"He died from the pox."

Elsa had tons of useless information stored in her head. There were two diseases people referred to as "the pox." She figured she'd ask about the one that wouldn't embarrass either one of them.

"Smallpox?"

He shook his head.

"Syphilis?" She wasn't sure how she felt knowing

a former resident died in her home from a venereal disease.

"No. Chickenpox."

Trenton walked inside carrying two boxes, one stacked on top of the other.

"Where would you like these, love?"

She warmed, hearing his term of endearment. They had become comfortable and familiar quickly. It was as if Trenton had come with the house. In some way, he did. This house was the start of everything good—or it would be the end of it.

"In the corner is fine." She turned back to Doc. "People die from chickenpox?"

Trenton headed for the door.

"Harvey did, right?"

Doc pointed at Trenton. "The boy has a brain like a steel trap."

As soon as the door closed, Doc said, "I take it he knows?"

She swallowed hard. "Yes. I take it *you* know?"

He nodded. "I'm your primary care manager. Dr. Trendle called me yesterday. I would have come over right away, but I figured you needed time to let it all soak in."

"I've absorbed it all right. It wasn't news I wanted, but I knew it was what I'd get."

Doc seemed to chew the inside of his cheek. "You know the saying, 'when life hands you lemons...'"

"Make a damn martini," she joked.

Doc's expression turned serious. "Did Dr. Trendle talk about your diagnosis and options?"

She could still hear Dr. Trendle's voice in her head. It played on repeat all night. "I have stage two cancer. She recommends I have the girls removed. My cancer is the type that responds well to hormone treatments so I might be able to avoid chemo." She ran her hand through her hair. "Marina just gave me a cut I like. I'd hate to lose my hair just when it's looking nice."

"Have you made a follow-up appointment?"

"She will hook me up with an oncologist. They will work together to heal me."

Doc gulped his coffee and set his mug on the table with a thud. "You seem to be taking it all well."

On the outside, she was a pillar of strength, but on the inside, she was quaking. "I allowed myself a pity party yesterday. There's no time to dwell on what I can't change." It was good self-talk, and she hoped she could benefit from her own wisdom.

"In my experience, you need to keep yourself busy." He looked over his shoulder at the boxes Trenton kept bringing inside. "It's good to have a project that will take your mind off your problems. And there's Trenton."

"Yes, there's Trenton." She glanced at the plastic cup of syrup and smiled. "He's actually very sweet."

"I don't know about sweet, but he appears to be a decent man. Keep him on his toes."

"I plan to."

Trenton walked in.

"This is the last box."

Doc gripped the edge of the table and used it to stand. "My job here is done." He shuffled to the door, but turned to face her. "Have you told the kids?"

She shook her head. "No, and I don't plan to."

"Why?" they said together.

She stood ramrod straight. "Because it's none of their business. Besides, their lives are complicated enough. They need to focus on their family and future."

"You are their family," Trenton said.

"I know, but..." She shook her head. "The answer is no."

Doc grumbled, but she couldn't pick out the words. She imagined he was telling her it was a big mistake to keep such a big secret, but it was her call. She wanted her kids to focus on life, not something that could cause death.

When the door closed, Trenton walked toward her.

"You have to tell them, love."

"Maybe."

"No maybes about it. They need to know."

She exhaled loudly, hoping he'd get the idea that she didn't want to discuss it anymore.

"It's my story to tell, and I'll tell it when I'm ready. Don't spill the beans."

"I won't." He crossed his heart.

"Good."

"Now what?" he asked, looking to the boxes in the corner.

"That can wait." She ran her finger down the buttons of his shirt. She always thought that looked seductive on the big screen. It felt sexy, but maybe that was because she knew what was in her head. Her breasts had a shelf life that was expiring and right now, all she wanted was to feel alive. "I thought I'd introduce you to the girls."

"The girls?"

She pointed to her breasts. "Yes, the girls." She turned and sashayed toward the bedroom. "One is sore because of the biopsy, but the other is ready to play." She exaggerated the sway of her hips and hoped it looked sexy. For all she knew, it looked like she was working an arthritis pain out of her joint. "Don't forget the syrup."

CHAPTER FOURTEEN

They laid in bed facing each other. He was happy for the introduction, and he'd miss the girls when they were gone, but they didn't define the woman who just rocked his world. Elsa was more than a pair of mammary glands.

His hand rested on her bare hip.

"Wow," he said. "That was ... unexpected."

"If I've learned anything this week, it's that life is unpredictable."

She shifted and her hair fell over her face until he brushed it back.

"You're beautiful." He traced the fine lines at the corner of her eye and ran his thumb down her cheek to touch her lips. "How do you do it?"

"Do what?"

"Stay so calm in the midst of a storm."

She laughed. "You have a short memory. Don't forget that I had a good cry yesterday. Today is a new day. We all have challenges. On some level, I feel blessed to know what mine will be."

"The outlook is good though?" He was so worried because now that he'd found her, he might lose her.

"From what they told me, it is. I haven't put my librarian hat on and researched yet. It seemed too daunting yesterday but today it's doable." She ran her hand up his bare chest to his neck and then cupped his cheek. "I understand if you want to run. I really do, but I hope you'll stay."

He kissed her and pulled back.

"I'm not going anywhere."

Her eyes lit up when she smiled. He recognized that smile as mischief in the making.

"Oh yes, you are. You're going to Maisey's to get pie while I heat the Indian food."

"You're very bossy."

She shrugged and fell to her back. "I'm used to being on my own and having things done my way."

He sat up and grabbed for his pants. "So am I. Will we butt heads?"

She stared at him for a moment. "Not as long as you're reasonable."

He stood and tugged on his jeans. "Let me guess, reasonable means you get your way most of the time."

"The first time I saw you, I thought, now there's a smart man."

She swung her legs off the bed and walked naked to the closet, where she took a silky embroidered robe from the hanger. He hated to see her cover up because she was living art. A master's stroke of a brush made every curve and dip. She was Rubens, Picasso, van Gogh, and Rembrandt all in one. The flimsy lush material clung to her body and didn't diminish the experience of being with Elsa.

"Just cherry pie?" He tugged on his shirt and started buttoning. "Were you serious about me staying here?"

She walked to him. "I don't want to rope you into becoming my caretaker, but I like that you're here. Besides, I have boxes of stuff to go through and since you have a history with this town, you could be an asset."

He lowered himself and wrapped his arms around her waist. When he stood, he lifted her from the ground.

"I can give you the villain's point of view."

She kicked her feet and shook her head. "You're no villain. In many ways, we are both alike. We are wounded and misunderstood."

He nuzzled into her neck.

"You want me here because I understand you?"

"No, I need you here. You have no idea how much that pains me to admit."

He let her slide down his front until her feet touched the ground.

"There is no weakness in needing someone."

"It's not something I'm used to. I'm very private. I don't like people to know my business."

He stood back and slipped on his shoes. Who needed socks when he'd be out and back in no time?

"Is that why you won't tell your kids?"

She turned and walked away. "Don't pressure me."

"I'm not. I just don't understand." He followed her into the living room, where she sat in the comfy chair.

"I know my kids, and I can't be a rock for them when I'm coming to terms with this myself. Although I knew there was something wrong, it's a very different situation when you get the diagnosis. Until then it was a maybe, and now it's definite."

He had so much to say about her keeping this from her kids, but now wasn't the time.

He checked his pockets for his wallet and his keys. Finding them there, he kissed her on the head.

"I'll be back soon." He walked out the door, filled with many emotions. He was happy to be with Elsa and so relieved she needed him. His ex-wife only needed his money. There was also fear that prickled at his senses. Was it smart to get involved with a woman in such a vulnerable place?

He pulled out of the driveway and asked himself if he could leave and never come back, and the answer was no. He needed Elsa too. Maybe more than she needed him.

HIS FIRST STOP was Maisey's. As he walked inside, the smell of bacon and French fries swirled around him.

"Back for something else?" Maisey leaned on the counter. Stereotypical of the small diner waitress, she snapped her gum and sipped from a lipstick-stained mug.

"Elsa wants cherry pie."

"That girl's a good wrapper."

He did not know what Maisey meant and wasn't sure he wanted clarification, but curiosity got the best of him.

"I don't follow."

Maisey boxed up a couple of slices of pie. "I wouldn't have taken you to be one of the slow ones. What I meant was Elsa didn't take any time getting you wrapped around her finger. First you come for breakfast and now for pie?"

He lifted a brow. Would that be how the entire town saw him—wrapped around Elsa's finger?

At some point in his life, he stopped caring about what people thought. Maybe it was because they always thought so poorly of him. He'd grown a thick skin over the years.

"Maybe I'm wooing her with your blue-plate specials, your amazing pancakes and your pie."

Maisey bagged up the pie and handed it to him. "That will do it. Add in some flowers occasionally, and you may have a chance of keeping a woman like her."

"What do I owe you for the pie and advice?"

"Both are on the house today. How's that arm of hers? I heard she was seeing someone in Copper Creek. It's not getting worse, is it?"

Small town gossip traveled fast, but the one thing about gossip was it was rarely accurate. You tell one guy your neighbor bought a Ford truck and by the time it gets back to you, he's driving a Maserati.

"I'm not her doctor, but she doesn't seem to be in any pain." That was true. Elsa was adjusting to her cast. It might take him a while longer because each time she laid her arm over him, it landed with a thud and was followed by an "I'm sorry, dang thing is heavy." His chest might have a bruise until her cast is gone.

"Tell her to call if she needs anything."

"I'll let her know."

He left with the pie in hand and walked to The Corner Store, where Beth was stocking the candy aisle.

"Coming back home finally?"

"Are you taking over as my mother?" He laughed. "I'm the last person you want to practice parenting on."

"If I were practicing parenting, you would have been turned over my knee twice by now."

"You're not going to be a 'spare the whip and spoil the child' mom?"

"There's a time and place for everything."

"You're right. And right now, it's time for me to get your mom some flowers." He walked to where several pots hung from a wire stand. There were bunches of daisies and carnations and roses. The selection was quite nice for a small store. "What does she like?"

Beth stopped loading the candy bars onto shelves and looked at him.

"She's not that particular."

"We're talking about your mom here. She's particular about everything from how her books are ordered to how her Chinese food gets put on the plate."

"Don't let the savory run into the sweet," Beth said. "You're paying attention. I wouldn't have expected that from you."

"Because I'm Mr. Van der Mean?" He glanced at the flowers again.

"She told you?"

He smiled. "Your mom and I don't have time for secrets. We ain't getting any younger."

Beth frowned. "Get her the daisies. She likes their simple elegance."

He removed all the daisy bouquets he could find and set them on the counter. "I'll be right back. I need to get my bag."

"What do you mean, get your bag?"

"Your mother has asked me to stay."

She gasped. "My mother would never have you stay. She's far too practical."

He climbed the stairs and picked up the bag of clothes he'd brought to Aspen Cove, and when he returned to the store, Beth was on the phone.

"I'm serious, Merrick. He says he's moving in with mom. Can't you do something? You're the sheriff." She obviously didn't like his response because she hung up with a harrumph.

She rang up the flowers. "I'll be keeping my eye on you."

He smiled. "I'm so happy Elsa's children are fierce like her. How could you be anything else?"

Beth's rigid shoulders softened. "She'll love the flowers."

"Thank you for your help."

"Don't be surprised if my brother runs a check on you."

He chuckled. "I wouldn't expect anything less than a thorough background check." He paid for the flowers and walked toward the door.

"You're not so bad," Beth said.

"I keep trying to tell everyone I'm not the villain."

"Don't forget that I've got a house that needs to be sold. It was one of your slums."

He almost forgot that Elsa was living in Beth's house, and now it was vacant.

"Call Mason, he'll hook you up."

It took him only a few minutes to return to Elsa, but he felt like he'd been gone a lifetime.

With pie in one hand and the flowers in the other, he tapped the door with his foot. While he would stay with her, it wasn't a permanent invite and he didn't want to assume he could walk in without permission.

She answered the door fully dressed.

"You could have walked in." She looked at the flowers. "For me? I love daisies."

"I heard."

She smiled. "Beth."

"Yes, and don't be surprised if she calls and tells you you've stayed out past curfew, or you've had enough sweets for the day."

She took the flowers and moved toward the kitchen.

"She already called."

"And Merrick?" He set the pie on the counter.

"He's already run a background check on you and says your record is as clean as a whistle. I expected no less."

"How would you know?"

She lifted on tiptoes and kissed him.

"I'm an excellent judge of character."

The air was filled with aromatic herbs and coconut curry.

"You're also a good warmer-upper. That smells amazing."

She picked up two prepared plates and walked into the living room, where she'd spread some contents of the boxes on the table.

"Did you know there was a brothel in town?"

CHAPTER FIFTEEN

"I think it was the best kept secret in town," he said. "Do you know where it was located?"

She took a seat on the sofa, and he sat beside her.

"No idea. It says something about Main Street, but I'm sure the town has changed over the years."

He took a bite of his tikka masala and moved the items on the table around until he came across a photo.

"Wow, who knew this was all here." He pointed to a wooden building.

The pictures showed a town with wooden sidewalks and structures and a dirt road. Horses were tied to posts, and a wagon was filled with what looked like sacks.

"This is only the first box I opened." While she

waited for him to return, she took the lid off the first box. She knew better than to look inside. The woman who loved words and stories couldn't resist the urge to dig deeper into the town's history. Doc had pegged her perfectly.

Trenton picked up the photo and pointed to a building. "This was once the saloon. It's now the sheriff's office." He chuckled. "Seems fitting, since the law could always be found there, anyway."

She stared at him. "You're telling me the sheriff's office was once a whorehouse?"

He shrugged. "Well, it was the saloon and a pleasure palace for those who drank in the sins of the flesh." He pointed to the building two doors down. "What's now Bishop's Brewhouse was once the mercantile."

"But now there's The Corner Store," she said

"Exactly. That was where my family came in. They always had an eye for property. It made little sense to put the busiest store in the center of town. That meant a lot of wagons on horses creating a bottleneck of sorts that blocked the road." He smiled. "Back in the day, there wasn't much here but a saloon, a sheriff's office, the mercantile and a livery."

"What about a doctor?"

"Aspen Cove never had one until Doc Parker." He shrugged. "My grandparents told me stories about how the doctor from Silver Springs would come through every few months to see chronic cases." He chuckled. "If I remember correctly, there was a woman who thought she was a healer. Everyone went to her until they found out she was no better than one of those guys selling snake oil at the circus."

"How did they know?" History fascinated her. Especially if she could see the growth. To look at the brick sheriff's office and know that it once was a brothel blew her mind.

"She was related to the old moonshiner who lives on the hill. I think it was his grandmother. People rarely felt well, but they didn't care because a pint of her shine made them forget they were sick."

"I've heard about him. I think his name is Zachariah."

"Sounds about right. The Tuckers were hill folk and had their own set of rules. I don't think any of them were properly educated."

Speaking of education." She rummaged through the papers and found a property deed. "Did you know that the Dawsons, who have also been here forever, donated land for a schoolhouse?"

He nodded. "It's on his land. Right at the edge of the property. It's just a pile of rotted lumber now. When we were kids, we used to sneak over there at night and drink the moonshine."

She held up the deed. "I wonder if this is still good?"

"Probably. I can't imagine them taking it back." He cocked his head. "What are you thinking?"

She took a bite of food and chewed while she decided if her thought was valid or silly.

"Doc seems to think the town would appreciate a museum of sorts. Maybe down the road, we can do some fundraisers like they did for the fire department and build something on the site."

He frowned. "You still got the hots for Lloyd?"

She leaned over to bop him with her shoulder. "Lloyd is a nice man. I've actually been out with him once. We went to the diner and had fried chicken."

"You've been on a date with him?"

She smiled. Trenton Van der Veen, wealthy and handsome, was jealous of a cowboy.

"It wasn't a date. We met at Thanksgiving. The town had a big gathering, and I came up from Denver to join. He was kind."

"I bet he was."

She nudged him again. "Hey, he's never seen me naked."

Trenton grinned. "No?"

She shook her head. "Nope. I reserve that privilege for charming property tycoons who make lousy real estate deals."

"Hey, it was a good deal for you."

She looked around her house. She practically stole it from him.

"It was."

He set his nearly-empty plate to the side and placed his hand on her knee.

"In the end, it turned out to be a pretty good deal for me."

She certainly was in a predicament. How did she move forward when half of her life felt like it was just beginning, and the other half was on a downward spiral?

"I think you got the booby prize."

He stared at her until she realized what she'd said. Her hand went to her mouth and covered her laughter.

"Are we really going there?"

While it wasn't funny, it kind of was. Humor had been her savior more than once, and she was sure her mind was on autopilot.

"Hey, I have to be able to joke about it. If I didn't, I might not get out of bed."

"Don't be a boob." He grinned. "Staying in bed sounds like a fabulous plan."

"I guess we're going there." She sat up straight, but her shoulders were already shaking from a pent-up laugh. "I'll keep you abreast in case I change my mind about staying in bed."

"You're an amazing woman." His eyes softened. "I don't know what you want or need, but all you have to do is ask."

She set her plate down and leaned against his shoulder. "You're here and that's all I could hope for." She turned to him and smiled. "How are you at doing the dishes?"

He raised his hand. "My first job was at Bob's Big Boy bussing tables, which included washing dishes."

That didn't make sense because he came from a long line of real estate moguls.

"I thought your family owned most of Colorado."

He laughed while he rose and walked the dishes to the sink.

"Oh, they were. But everyone in the family had to work a job outside of the family empire. It was my father's and his father's way of showing us how the other half lived."

"Did you hate it?"

He plugged the sink, turned on the water and added some dish soap.

"No, I loved it. Imagine living with your family and working with them. Going to the triple B was like going to summer camp. I got to meet people, eat greasy food, and enjoy autonomy. Being a Van der Veen is a way of life."

She leaned against the counter and watched as he scrubbed the dishes, rinsed them, and put them on a towel to dry.

"I can't imagine. Did you raise your son that way?"

He frowned. "No, I gave him everything and when I realized I'd given him too much, I took it all away. That's how he ended up here. I wasn't sure if that would be the best or worst decision."

"It turned out all right. He seems happy."

Trenton nodded. "Yep, and I'm incredibly proud. He was willing to walk away from it all for love. I was never that brave."

"You seem pretty valiant now." He'd left everything he had in Denver to come up to Aspen Cove to get closer to his son and her. That took courage.

"I wouldn't call it bravery as much as I'd call it desperation."

Her eyes widened. "Explain."

"Imagine being around hundreds of people every day and feeling lonely. My life was a carefully erected facade. I had money and cars and houses, but I had nothing in my heart. I was very much like the mansion I lived in—cold and lifeless."

She raised her hand. "I know exactly what you were going through." She snickered. "Although I didn't have the cars and houses. I had two children who filled my heart, but they never warmed my bed." She turned around and took out two plates from the cupboard. "And they were terrible dishwashers."

"Then you've upgraded."

She wanted to smile but couldn't.

"You know, I definitely upgraded, but what about you? I might not be what you bargained for."

He opened the Styrofoam container that held the pieces of pie. "Best dog I ever had was missing an eye."

She drew in a sharp breath. "You did not just compare me to your dog."

He shook his head. "No." He placed the pie on the plates and faced her. "Life is challenging. And you ... are far more than I bargained for."

Her heart sank. "I get it."

He tipped her chin up with his thumb. "No, you don't. I was married to a woman who appeared perfect on the outside, but she was hollow on the inside. There was nothing of substance. I swear she had more filler than feelings. You, on the other hand, are a passionate woman. You are sharing your life and experiences with me. You're as brave as they come." He looked at her chest. "Will I miss the girls?" He smiled. "Sure, it was lovely to meet them, but they are not what define who Elsa Buchanan is." He laid his hand between her breasts. "You have to dig deeper into her heart to see that."

"Are you trying to get into my bed again?"

He leaned down and brushed his lips against hers. "No, I want inside your heart. I can't imagine anyone you let in there ever wanting to leave."

She considered the men in her life.

"If we're being honest, I've never met a man who ever wanted to stay."

He held out his hand. "I'm Trenton Van der Veen, it's nice to meet you."

"I'm glad you're here," she said.

He picked up the plates of pie and walked into the living room.

"Me too. And don't forget, if you need anything, just tell me."

She sat on the couch and looked at the boxes piling up in the corner.

"Right now, I need pie and then I'll need help to catalogue all of that." She chewed her lip. "And a couple of rides back to Copper Creek. My surgery will be in two weeks."

He took what seemed like a lifetime to take that in. She wasn't sure if he was changing his mind or simply processing.

"Just give me the dates and your chariot will await, but don't let me step on any toes. I'm sure your kids will want to be there too."

He always brought up the kids and maybe she was crazy not telling them.

"Trenton," she warned. "These are my breasts."

"Yes, sweetheart, I know, but those are your kids, too. What would you do if Beth was going through the same thing and didn't tell you? Besides, she needs to know. It could be hereditary."

She hated that he made valid points, but both of her kids were expecting kids. This was supposed to be a time of joy and excitement.

She let out an exasperated breath. "You're right, but it will be on my terms. Besides, 'I've got cancer' is a mood buster." She shifted the papers on the table. "Did you know that Buffalo Bill came through town?"

Trenton sat back and smiled. "He probably came for the brothel."

"Or a new horse. There was a reason there was a livery in town. There was also a blacksmith that made horseshoes and wedding rings."

"You learned all of this while I was gone?"

"I was very good at what I did."

"It's no wonder why Doc saddled you with the job."

"I'm tenacious." She waved her hand in the air. "I'll have this whipped into shape in no time, but I'll probably need help with finding a place to display it."

"Maybe you can sweet talk Lloyd into building you a new schoolhouse."

He watched for her reaction and because she didn't enjoy being baited, she pushed back.

"It might require more kisses."

Trenton lifted his brows.

"I'll do the negotiating with Lloyd."

"I thought so." She took a bite of pie.

CHAPTER SIXTEEN

The next day, Trenton headed toward the Big D
Ranch. He had nothing bad to say about Lloyd. He
hardly remembered the man from his visits. He knew
their family had long ties with Aspen Cove. Not a
founding member, but shortly after the first residents
moved in.

The thing about the ranchers was they stuck to
themselves, so all Trenton knew was Lloyd raised
cattle and had a bunch of girls named after flowers
and a boy named after a spice of some sort.

He parked near the house, where he spotted
Lloyd sitting on the porch. He killed the engine and
stepped out.

"What brings you to my ranch?" Lloyd asked.

Elsa brought him to the ranch. He didn't want

her hanging out with Lloyd. Though she told him she wasn't interested in the man, they had what he'd call a date and they shared a kiss. Sharing might be stretching the truth a bit because it appeared that Elsa stole the kiss.

"I wanted to talk to you about a land deed."

Lloyd narrowed his eyes. "I'm not selling my land. Your grandfather already tried to run my family off once. It's not happening."

Trenton held his hands up as if he surrendered.

"No, not this land." He reached into his pocket and pulled out the folded document. "Years ago, the land where the dilapidated schoolhouse sits belonged to your family, and you deeded it to the city so they could use the space to build a school."

Lloyd rubbed his whiskers. "That's right. That isn't for sale either."

"I'm not trying to buy it." He hated he had to carry decades of his family's misdeeds on his shoulders. "I'm not my grandfather." People thought Trenton was the devil, but his grandfather was ten times worse. He would have been waiting on a person's porch with a contract if he thought there was a chance they'd die overnight. While Trenton drove a hard bargain, he at least tried to be human. That was what turned all this around. He'd been less than a good human to his son, and while the lesson was a good one, he learned more from it than he ever hoped to teach Mason. His son taught him that loyalty and love should always come first.

Lloyd rose from his chair and walked down the steps, his heavy boots thumping hard on the wood.

"You may not be your grandfather, or your father, but in my experience, the calf doesn't move far from the milk."

Trenton wanted to laugh but feared he'd offend Lloyd.

"I'm lactose intolerant."

"Why do you care about the property?"

"I don't." If putting historical documents on a site that's historical and was once used for learning made little sense, then he wouldn't be here. "Elsa does."

Lloyd looked down at the ground and kicked the dirt until a low cloud formed.

"Elsa, huh?" He leaned over to where the grass had grown tall by the steps and plucked out a long blade, sticking it in the corner of his mouth. "That's a mighty fine woman there."

A knot of jealousy twisted in Trenton's gut. He wasn't much of a caveman, but he didn't like another man thinking about his woman in that way, even if it was true. Elsa was mighty fine.

"She is a wonderful woman."

Lloyd nodded. "I've spent some time with her. She has all the qualities a man would find attractive."

Lloyd seemed to bait him, but he wasn't certain.

The last thing he needed was to fight with the one man who could make things work out for the historical museum. But if he pushed Trenton too far, he'd figure out a way to buy the land, regardless.

Right then, he resembled his father and grandfather. They'd stop at nothing to get what they wanted. At this point in his life, all he wanted was Elsa and a relationship with his son.

Trenton passed the deed to Lloyd.

"As you know, Doc enlisted Elsa's help to catalogue and organize the town's history. According to one of those documents, the schoolhouse was deeded to the town. All I need to know is if the deed is still valid. Was there another agreement after this that nullifies this deed?"

"No, the schoolhouse still belongs to the town, as does the land. The Dawsons don't take back what they give."

Trenton was sure that was some jab against his family, but wasn't sure which event spurred it.

"Then we can use the property for the historical museum."

Lloyd chewed on his blade of grass. "You've seen the schoolhouse, right? It's rubble. Nothing is going there."

"I've seen it. It can be rebuilt."

"With Van der Veen money?" He shook his head. "I don't think that's a good idea."

"Who cares whose money it is. All that matters is it gets done and soon."

Lloyd went back to moving dirt and gravel with his boot. "I care because I don't want there to be an issue in a year or two or ten. I don't want my grand-children having to fight you over it."

Trenton closed his eyes and took a deep, cleansing breath.

"Tell you what, how about I write you a big fat check and you pay for the rebuild? That way it can be a gift from the Dawsons."

Lloyd's eyes narrowed to slits. "That's not like you."

Trenton threw his hands into the air. "How would you know? You don't even know me."

The boot scraping stopped. "Tell you what. How about you donate the money to the city, which would be Doc, and he can distribute the funds for refur-bishment?"

Trenton smiled. "Have you seen that building? It's not a refurb project. It's a rebuild."

The smile on Lloyd's face told Trenton that Lloyd was warming up to him.

"You could contact the Cooper brothers. They've done a lot of work in town with their green-house projects. Sustainable building is a thing." He looked over his shoulder toward his home. "You won't catch me living in one, but lots of people like them and it would show that Aspen Cove is energy conscious."

He had to give the cowboy credit. That was a good idea.

"I'll call them. Thank you."

Lloyd held out his hand, and Trenton shook it.

"Be good to Elsa. If I was in the market for a companion, she would have been my choice."

Trenton hung his head. "I'm sorry about your loss. I can't imagine how hard it would be to lose your soul mate."

Lloyd smiled. "Let's hope you never have to find out. Rips your heart out and takes your soul with it."

"Thank you for the chat," Trenton said.

"Thanks for not being like your ancestors."

Trenton laughed. "Oh, you were right. The calf doesn't move far from the milk. I was just like them, but I'm turning over a new leaf."

"My pop always told me that reflection was the first stage of redemption. I hope you spend a lot of time thinking about what you want."

He pointed to himself. "Watch this old dog learn new tricks."

Lloyd handed him the deed back. "Let me know if you need any help."

Trenton shook his head. "Just stay away from my girl." While he said it with humor in his voice, he meant it. Now that he and Elsa had shared intimate moments, not only was his body committed, but she'd taken over his heart and mind.

Lloyd turned toward the barn and waved his hand in the air.

"See you around."

Trenton took his seat and drove down the long, winding dirt road that led to town. He reached Lake Circle and took in the cabins that lined the water. One stuck out. Not that it didn't blend in, because it did, but it wasn't familiar.

He pulled into the driveway, and out walked the owner.

Trenton parked the car and exited.

"Can I help you?" the man asked.

"Yes, I'm Trenton Van der Veen, and I was wondering about your house."

The man smiled. "I'm Luke." He turned to face the home. "It's a beauty, isn't it?"

Trenton had to admit that it was a nice-looking house. The lines were clean and blended right in with the other homes on the lake.

"Who's the builder?"

"Cooper Construction. Let me get their card." He disappeared into the house and was back less than a minute later. "They have all kinds of styles. Just tell them what you want, and they can have it up in weeks."

Trenton's head snapped back. "Weeks?"

"It's a kit. There are several in town. It's hard to pick them out because they blend right in, but they have running water, indoor plumbing, and they cost nothing to power."

Trenton looked at the card. The company was from Frazier Falls, which wasn't too far from Aspen Cove.

"Thanks, I'll call them."

As soon as he was in his car, he called his son.

"Mason, this is Dad."

"What's up?" In the background, a saw buzzed.

"Have I caught you at a bad time?"

There was a moment of silence. "Are you living next door now?"

It almost slipped his mind that Jewel and Mason lived in the home next door. They were never there. He figured they were refurbing the remaining houses.

"I am. I'd love to spend some time with my son."

Again, the silence ate up a few seconds—seconds that felt like hours. "What's going on with you? You're not terminal or anything, are you? I mean ... most people don't go from old Scrooge to new Scrooge overnight."

"I'm not sick." He thought about Elsa and wondered if she'd change because of her diagnosis. He hoped not. He liked her the way she was. "But I had a change of heart. I've looked at my past, and I'm adjusting my present so I can have a better future."

"I'm glad."

"How's Jewel?"

"Dad, she's amazing. It's surprising how much the right woman can fill your life with joy."

While he didn't want to comment because Mason's mother was not the joy-inducing woman he thought she'd be, he didn't want to say so and offend his son. All boys should love their mother.

"I'm glad you've found true love."

"What about you?"

What did he tell his son? "I'm happier than I've been in a very long time."

"You know what, Dad? I'm glad. I know you guys stayed together for many reasons but bad is bad and there's no reason to make each other miserable."

"I'm glad you understand. Have you spoken to your mother?" He truly didn't care what she was up to but asking seemed polite.

"Yes, I think she's going to marry her yoga instructor."

He started toward home. It was funny to think of the little bungalow as home, but it wasn't the house that made it feel like that. It was Elsa.

"She always had a thing for the athletic types. Anyway, son, I called to ask if you'd like the commission for a home kit the town is going to buy for the new historical museum."

"We're getting a historical museum?"

"Yes, and I thought if there was any finish work, maybe Jewel might want to be involved."

"How are you involved?"

He pulled in the driveway and sat behind the wheel.

"I fell for a librarian."

"Do you think you could love her?"

Trenton smiled. "I think I already might."

"I'm glad, Dad. I'm happy to broker the deal, but don't you want the commission?"

"Mason, all I care about is you and Elsa. Money isn't even on my radar any longer."

"Wow." He could almost see his son smile. "Let's meet for a beer later at the Brewhouse and we can talk about it. Will that be okay?"

He exited the car and started for the door. "That'll be perfect."

He hung up and instead of knocking, he walked inside the house like Elsa had told him to.

"Honey, I'm home."

CHAPTER SEVENTEEN

Elsa looked around her home. Where had the time gone? It had been over a week since Trenton moved in. A week of bliss. He was everything she thought he'd be and more. Sometimes too much when he fussed over her. She wasn't used to that, but couldn't say she didn't like it.

"I got salmon and chicken breasts," he called from the kitchen. The kids were coming for dinner and Trenton went shopping in Copper Creek. He brought home half the store and a barbecue.

"We aren't feeding an army," she said.

"Have you seen your son? What about Gray? It's not like he's a little man. Then there are the girls; they're both pregnant."

She moved behind him and wrapped her arms around his waist. "You're a good man, Trenton. Your ex-wife was an idiot to let you go."

He turned around to face her.

"I'm a bad man who's trying to be better. As for my ex ... we were like oil and water." He chuckled. "Actually, we were worse. More like she was gasoline, and I was fire. In the right circumstances, we worked well together, but our relationship turned into a perpetual disaster."

"Then why did you marry her?" She had a lot of questions for the man in front of her. She'd peppered him with them over the last week but had stayed away from his past relationship because it didn't seem fair to bring up such a recent wound, but curious minds wanted to know.

"She was beautiful and acceptable to my family. We came from the same stock."

She cocked her head. "You sound like you're buying cattle."

He rocked back and forth. "It was more like horses. When you come from an affluent family, all they care about is breeding and pedigree. In my family, you didn't marry for love but for connections. My ex was a thoroughbred in our circles."

"Maybe you *are* Mr. Darcy. In his time, they married for wealth."

Trenton turned back to the counter and unpacked the bags. "Back then, women had dowries and everything that belonged to her before the marriage now belonged to him after."

"Archaic," she said

"It's not much different. You come into a relationship with whatever you have. You leave it with half."

"She took half?"

He shook his head.

"No, I *gave* her half. At the end of the day, like you said, you never need more than enough. Even at half, it's more than enough."

"I had dreams of marriage in the day. I wanted to have the white wedding and the flowers, but it never came to pass. I guess on some level, I'm a force to be reckoned with. Maybe I'm too prickly. Living with me is like living with a porcupine."

"My favorite animal." He spun around and kissed her.

When he pulled away, he stared into her eyes. "You're stubborn, but you're a good woman."

"How have I shown you I'm good? All you've seen is the bad. I tampered with my kids' lives. I pretty much stole this house from you. I'm ill." She raised her hand. "And I clobber you at least once a day with my cast."

"Do you do it on purpose?"

She shook her head. There was a time or two where he could use a good clobbering, but she wasn't that cruel.

"No, I just forget about it."

"Accidents don't make you a bad person."

She'd been feeling very guilty lately about a lot of things.

"Okay, but what about the house? I basically stole it."

He laughed.

"Honey, do you think I wasn't aware of what was going on? I wanted you to have the house. I would have given it to you if you had pressed a little harder."

"But you didn't know me then."

He set his hands on her shoulders. "I've been an excellent judge of character all my life, and you, Elsa Buchanan, are a character."

She leaned into him and placed her head on his chest.

"You should invite Mason and Jewel to dinner."

He rubbed her back. "This is an opportunity to get to know your family. There will be time for big gatherings later."

Deep inside, she knew that to be true. These days, having breast cancer wasn't an immediate death sentence, but it did give her pause and make her think about how she'd conducted her life.

She'd allowed two men into her heart, and both had shredded it to pieces. Trenton was chipping at the stone exterior and working his way in. Oh hell, who was she kidding? He'd started in her heart and was chipping at the outer wall from the inside. They were peas from the same pod. Good mostly, but often misunderstood. She understood him.

"What can I do to help?" The kids were coming in an hour.

"I've got it under control. Pull up a chair and talk to me."

She did as he asked. "Do you know what my idea of foreplay is?"

He started chopping tomatoes.

"Coffee and a first edition of Pride and Prejudice in bed?"

"That would do it, but this is nice, too. Outside of Merrick cooking dinner once a week, I've never had a meal made by a man."

"Don't get your hopes up too high, I can barbecue and make a salad." He nodded to the other bags on the counter. "The rest is ready-made. All I have to do is heat and serve."

She smiled. "It's still sexy."

He picked up a chunk of tomato and pressed it to her lips.

"If we had more time, I'd stop this foreplay, and start something far more gratifying."

A shiver ran down her body. She knew what that man could do to her. All he had to do was say, "Are you ready for bed?" Those five words sent her into overdrive. She'd always heard that women as they aged lost their sex drive. With Trenton, she felt like a much younger woman.

They spent hours satisfying each other. That wasn't quite the truth. Trenton spent hours pleasing her and in turn he gained satisfaction, knowing he could rock her world. She only hoped that she could keep him happy as well.

"Are you content here?" She chose her words wisely because happy was fleeting or it had been in her experience, but content could last a long time.

"Content?" He put down the knife and squatted in front of her. "I don't think you understand what being with you means. I'm ecstatic. You're a beautiful, intelligent woman who doesn't need me but allows me to need her."

She hated to admit to any man that she needed him, but Trenton deserved to know the truth.

"I need you, and that scares me."

"You've got a lot of scary things going on."

It was true. She had a broken wrist, a lump in her breast, and a man who was proving to be so much more than she bargained for.

"I can handle all the medical stuff." She said the words out loud, and they felt true. She could handle them. She'd handled worse. Hell, she rescued a library full of people when a suicidal man pulled a gun. Most people would crumble after that. She wasn't a quake in the face of fear kind of woman. She was a fall apart afterward when she was alone kind of gal.

"What don't you think you can handle?" He cupped her cheek. "What scares you?"

She took several breaths. "That one day, you'll wake up next to me and ask yourself ... what in the hell was I thinking? I have nothing to offer you. In fact, I'm fairly certain your family would think my pedigree lacking. I'm Heinz 57—a mix of a bunch of stuff."

He reached toward the table and pulled a chair toward them and took a seat.

"I like a bunch of stuff. Have you ever had one of those spinach salads with the nuts and cranberries?"

She stared at the ingredients on the counter, wondering if he was talking about that.

"Yes."

"That's just proof that when you have a variety of things mixed, it has the potential to make something special. Spinach alone is fine, but it's better with all the extras. They bring texture and flavor and sweetness to the bland vegetable."

"Are you comparing me to a spinach salad?"

He nodded. "Yes, I am. Your mixture is the exact flavor I love."

"You love me?" She didn't expect him to admit it. She wasn't even sure it was possible. She'd been telling herself that it was too soon for those feelings, but she'd be damned if she wasn't feeling it too. At first, she thought it was a case of heartburn with the way her chest squeezed each time they were together. Then, each time he left the house, there was a major void she'd never felt before. Even her collection of old classics and her corner chair weren't as comfortable. She'd rather be sitting in bed, watching TV, and eating out of the same popcorn bowl.

He stared at her for a few moments.

"You know what? As crazy as it seems, I think I love you. Love isn't supposed to happen like this, but maybe this is exactly how it happens. I always assumed that love was a slow burn, slow build kind of thing. You're more like a fast-moving fire. You swept over me, and I've been hot for you since."

"Hot for me, huh?"

"Yes, but not only that. I've had a lot of sex in my life, but it's not the same as making love. When I'm with you, all I care about is you and how you feel."

"You make me feel and that's far more than I could say for anyone else."

"Good. Now let's get this dinner finished because as soon as your kids leave, I'm going to make you feel really good."

That familiar thrill raced through her veins. She almost considered calling the dinner off because she wasn't sure she wanted to share Trenton with Merrick or Beth.

A half an hour later, someone knocked at the door and by the sound of it, she was certain it was Merrick. He was heavy fisted and made himself known whenever he came for a visit.

"Come in," Elsa said as she opened the door to find not only Merrick and Deanna, but Beth and Gray as well.

Deanna brought flowers while Beth brought a dessert. She was happy to see that Deanna came from the same school Beth did. The upbringing that taught you to never go to someone's house empty-handed. As for Elsa, she wouldn't have really cared, but knowing Deanna would raise her grandchild, she was happy the baby would have some manners. Dealing with everyone's offspring in the public libraries made her realize that most children were raising themselves and doing a poor job of it.

"Trenton has put together a feast for us." Just then, Trenton walked out of the kitchen, wiping his hands on a towel.

"Who's hungry?"

Deanna raised her hand. "I'm eating for two."

Merrick kissed her cheek and rubbed his hand over her stomach. "My girls need to eat regularly."

Elsa perked up. "Did you say girls as in Deanna and the baby?" She danced around the room and clapped her hands. "I'm getting one of each?"

Trenton laughed. "Couldn't have planned that one any better."

Beth and Deanna put their hands on their blossoming bellies.

"Oh, she planned it all right," they both said.

Beth looked at Trenton. "You understand what a menace my mother is, right?"

"Oh, I know, but I also know that most things worth having don't come easy."

"You're in the wrong shop if you're looking for that," Beth said. "The Buchanan name has never been synonymous with easy, but we are worth it." She turned and looked at Gray. "Isn't that right, honey?"

He nodded. "Just say yes and you'll never sleep on the couch."

Beth slugged him on the arm. "That's where you'll be sleeping tonight if you're not nice."

He tossed his hands in the air. "What? I agreed with you."

"You're impossible," Beth said, but lifted on tiptoes to kiss Gray. "Impossible not to love."

"I'm going to throw the meat on the grill."

Trenton nodded to the kitchen. "Does anyone want to join me?"

Merrick and Gray volunteered and followed Trenton to the back door. Just as he opened it, Elsa heard Merrick ask, "What are your intentions toward my mother?"

CHAPTER EIGHTEEN

"My current intentions are to feed her." He walked outside and opened the preheated grill. He was grateful the guy at the hardware store was willing to sell him the floor model, or they wouldn't have eaten until midnight.

He put the chicken on first since it would take longer to grill.

"I mean, what are your long-term plans for my mother?" Merrick asked.

"Yeah," Gray echoed. "Beth isn't your biggest fan, so don't do anything stupid to hurt Elsa."

Trenton was happy the boys were standing up for her. Everyone needed a champion and Elsa needed everyone she could get to stand behind her. He wished she would come clean about her surgery.

It only made sense to him to let them know, but it wasn't his story to tell, and he'd have to respect her wishes.

She only had a short time to let them know because she'd be in the hospital for a few days. They would wonder where she had disappeared to.

He looked at both men. "I'm falling in love with your mom." Although Gray wasn't technically related, he was the father of Beth's baby. "When are you going to marry Beth?"

Gray rolled his eyes. "She refuses to marry me until after our son is born. She wants to be skinny and look good." He shook his head. "I think she's gorgeous no matter what, but she's afraid the press might eat her alive."

Trenton looked at Merrick. "What about you?"

"Oh, I got that ring on her finger and the baby in her belly. That woman is all mine."

"I think your mother is feeling a little guilty about what she did."

Merrick leaned against the deck railing. "She's a meddler, but her heart is pure. I'm not mad at her. Shocked ... yes, but mad?" He shrugged. "How could I be? I have a little girl on the way and a beautiful wife. While my mother was being selfish, she gave me everything."

"I agree," Gray said. "However, I will warn you that the Buchanan women are stubborn."

Trenton laughed. "You think? I bet Elsa would argue that she's persistent and not stubborn."

Merrick laughed. "My mom would argue over everything. She's been the captain of her ship for so long that I'm pretty sure she doesn't know how to let anyone else take the helm. She's so afraid of running aground."

"I know that." He flipped the chicken and put the salmon on to cook.

"You don't come across as the type of guy who lets others take the reins."

Merrick was obviously worried about his mother. He'd used his position to run a background check on Trenton, but he couldn't hold that against him. It was what any son with those connections should do.

"You're right, but when you do the same thing and get the same results year after year, then you need to change. I am capable of change." He flipped the salmon.

"What about my mom's broken arm?" Merrick narrowed his eyes.

"Totally my fault."

Both men stared at him.

"I don't mean I snapped it myself, but I opened the door to the diner and let her enter first. I didn't see the wet floor, and I wasn't quick enough to catch her when she went down."

"That's not your fault. I'm going to tell you something about my mom, but you probably already know it. She'll never let you see her sweat. For some reason, she believes that if she shows you her pain or vulnerability, then she's less of a person." Merrick rubbed his jaw. "Since you are the one living with her, Beth and I will count on you to keep us in the know."

Trenton's stomach twisted.

"You need to let us know what's going on with her. She could be dying of cancer, and she'd never let us know. Promise me that if something is going on with her, you'll keep us in the loop."

Trenton turned and took the meat off the grill. "I think it's ready." He was game to be done with this conversation. He picked up the platter and headed to the door.

"Promise me, Trenton." Merrick said.

"I promise," he said before walking into the house. Now, what was he going to do? Merrick squeezed a promise out of him—a commitment he couldn't keep if Elsa continued to be hardheaded.

When he made it to the kitchen, he found that Elsa and the girls had extended the table and set it for dinner.

"That was fast," Elsa said. "I didn't even get to wheedle the babies' names out of the girls yet."

Deanna patted her stomach. "This is Aidy Buchanan."

Trenton watched Elsa's expression go from surprise to a smile. A second later, her eyes filled with tears.

"She would have loved that."

"Wait," Trenton said. "Who's Aidy?"

"Our grandmother," Beth said. "If you thought my mom was a fireball, you should have met Grandma Aidy."

"She's passed?" He wished he knew Elsa better.

"Yes." Elsa stared at him with what looked like a warning. "She had breast cancer."

His stomach lurched, and he swallowed the bitter bile that threatened to burn his tonsils.

"I'm sorry to hear that." He looked at the table, all set for a feast. "Shall we eat?" He wasn't in a position to ask her the questions he needed to. If her mother died from cancer, then it was probably hereditary, and that meant that Beth was at risk.

They sat around the table like a big family, and they were. He was the odd man out. Maybe he should have invited Mason and Jewel. There was enough food for all of them.

"What do you think grandma would have thought about being a great grandmother?" Beth asked.

Elsa laughed. "She would have had to come up with some cutesy name for the babies to call her. She didn't even let you two call her grandma in her presence."

"What did you call her?" Trenton asked.

"Ya-ya." Merrick rubbed his face. "I remember when she got sick. She refused to let them take her breasts."

Trenton took that in.

"I can understand that," Beth said. "She was a lingerie model in her day." She snorted. "And Madonna thought she was the first to come up with the cone bra. Ya-ya modeled those for Sears and Roebuck." She covered her mouth and laughed. "Mom would get the catalogue and tear those sections out, but Jeannie Franginelli always brought her copy to school. That's how I learned to fight."

"You fought over a catalogue?" Deanna asked.

"No, I punched Jeannie in the kisser for tacking my grandma's picture in the lunchroom. She never did it again and I found out I had a pretty good right hook."

Gray raised his hand. "I can attest to that. I've been the recipient of her right hook a time or two."

"Only in play." Beth took a sip of water. "I have to say, Ya-ya looked good in those thigh highs and pointy bra."

Trenton stared at Elsa. "Did she tell you right away, or did she keep it to herself?" It was a pinnacle question.

Elsa opened her mouth, but Beth chimed in.

"The day she got her diagnosis, she called a family meeting."

He continued to stare at Elsa, who looked like she was ready to crawl under the table.

"Who keeps a secret like that?" Deanna asked.

"Who indeed?" Trenton asked. He was torn between what he knew was right for her family and what he knew was right if he wanted to keep Elsa in his life. The problem was, he was screwed either way. If he kept Elsa's secret, then her kids would hate him. If he told her kids, then she would hate him. Either way, it meant he didn't have a chance in hell.

"Shall we have dessert?" Elsa asked. "Trenton picked up a cherry pie and vanilla ice cream."

She placed her hand on the table to rise, and he covered it.

"Please sit back down."

She cocked her head and her eyes got caught-in-the-headlights big. He could tell she was as frightened as a doe.

"Don't do it," she warned.

The room grew silent.

"Don't do what?" Merrick asked.

Elsa yanked her hand back. "Please don't."

"Honey, I have to. I made a promise to Merrick, and I refuse to let him down."

She looked at him with pleading eyes.

"But you made a promise to me, too. You said you wouldn't."

"You're right and I won't, but you have to."

She stood and stomped her foot. "You are manipulating me."

He nodded. "I am because you and I know it's the right thing to do."

"For whom?" she screamed.

"Everyone. They need to know."

Merrick slammed his palm on the table, sending the silverware skittering. "What in the hell is going on here?" He was a big man, well over six feet tall, and his presence was imposing on a normal day, but right then he looked downright deadly.

"Don't tell me you're pregnant too," Beth said.

Trenton imagined she was trying to lighten the air, but no one was paying attention.

Elsa sank into her seat.

"First, I want to say that I'm furious. I didn't get to choose the time and place to tell you. This is my story." She glared at Trenton.

"A story that you'd take to the grave if you could." He reached for her hand, but she yanked it away. "It's okay to let people in. It's okay to have weak moments. I love your strength, but geez, Elsa, let others bear the burden for a while."

"If someone doesn't start talking soon, I'll cuff

you all and lock you up until you do." Merrick's face was getting redder by the second.

Elsa waved him off. "That's not right and you know it. I taught you better."

Merrick cleared his throat. "You taught me to tell the truth."

"Fine," Elsa said. "I have breast cancer."

The entire room went silent.

"And you weren't going to tell us?" Beth asked.

"No, I didn't want to worry anyone. It's going to be fine. I'll have surgery and everything will be good."

Merrick shook his head.

"What were you going to do? Surely we would have asked where you were?"

She stared at Trenton. "I was going to tell you we were going away for a few days."

"Why?"

"Because of this. I can see the worry in your eyes, and you have enough on your plate that you don't need to worry about me. I can't be your rock when I need to be my own."

Beth gasped. "Oh my gosh, you've known for a long time. That's why you moved. You had no plans to tell us."

Elsa sighed. "I didn't know, but I had a feeling. And yes, I moved because if I needed chemo and lost my hair, or was looking gaunt, there was no way you wouldn't notice."

"I'll never understand you." She looked down at her stomach. "You knew when you poked holes in Merrick's condoms."

There was a collective gasp.

Elsa turned to Trenton. "See what you did?"

He knew he'd be the fall guy, but at least the truth was out there. "I wasn't the one withholding information. This is all on you."

Elsa stood and went to the counter to get the pie. "Let's have pie."

Deanna got up to help her, but Merrick asked her to stay.

"Mom, this isn't something that can be forgotten with pie. You're ill, and you weren't honest." He turned toward Trenton. "Thank you for being a man of your word."

Elsa grunted. "He didn't keep his word to me."

"Because I care about you, and if I'm to be a part of your life, I can't start it by lying to your kids."

"You're not sleeping with my kids," she said. "You owed me your loyalty."

Merrick covered his ears. "Come on, Mom. He's right, and you know it."

"He's not right, and *he* knows it."

Trenton pointed to himself. "He's right here."

Elsa pointed to the door. "I need you to leave."

Trenton knew that was coming. He rose and bent over to kiss the top of her head.

"I know you're mad at me. I hope you will find it in your heart to forgive me. They needed to know."

He swiped his keys off the counter and walked toward the door.

"Mom, are you going to just let him leave?"

CHAPTER NINETEEN

Trenton closed the door behind him, and Elsa responded to Beth's question.

"He betrayed me."

"He was looking out for you. If you didn't tell us, I might not have spoken to you again."

Elsa waved a hand of dismissal at Beth.

"Of course you'd talk to me. I'm your mother. You have to speak to me." The very thought of her kids not talking to her made her head spin.

"What?" Merrick asked. "There are different rules for different people? You were never a 'do as I say, not as I do' mom. You held us accountable for everything. If we lied or withheld the truth, we got the wooden spoon on our bottom." He huffed and folded his arms over his chest.

"That's right," Beth said. She pointed to the kitchen. "Get the spoon."

"I will not. I'm a grown woman."

Gray cleared his throat. "I may be out of line, but you're sure acting like a child."

Elsa stared at him, then looked at her daughter. "Does he talk to you like that?"

She shook her head.

"I didn't lie."

"Neither did I. Withholding information isn't a lie."

"That's semantics," Deanna said.

Elsa flopped against the seat. "You're all ganging up on me."

"No one is ganging up on you." Merrick palmed his face. "We need answers. Is it going to be like Ya-ya?"

"Do I have to worry?" Beth squeaked.

Elsa threw her hands into the air. "And that is why I said nothing. You will all worry."

Gray rubbed the whiskers on his chin. "Beth has a right to know what she's up against—what we're both up against."

She took several calming breaths. Part of her wanted to eat pie and forget about the C word. That was her inner child. The adult version of herself completely understood where her kids were coming from.

"Do you remember how hard we all took it when

Ya-ya told us?" She turned to Beth. "You cried for three days."

"I was sixteen."

It was true. She was an emotional teen. She looked at Merrick.

"You went on silent mode for a week."

"I was processing."

He leaned back, and the chair creaked. It was just a matter of time before he busted one of them. Elsa ran her hand over the wooden top. This was her mother's table. It held lots of memories and gum until she figured out that Merrick and Beth stuck it on the bottom side of the table when they sat down for dinner.

Once she figured that out, it took her a week to scrape it off.

"The point is that everyone took it badly."

"She was dying," Beth whined.

"No, honey, she was living the way she chose. She didn't want to lose her breasts. She tried chemo, but the quality of her life was so poor that she didn't want to spend the rest of her life dying. She wanted to live."

"Ya-ya's cancer was advanced when she found it. Where is yours?" Merrick asked. Nothing like a cop to get to the bottom of things quickly.

"It's early, and I'm opting to have both breasts removed so there's little chance of the other one becoming involved. It's treatable through hormone therapy. I won't have to have chemo."

"See how easy that was?" Beth asked. "You told us, and no one is losing their mind."

"I know you." She watched as the tears pooled in her daughter's eyes. "You've got about thirty seconds before the floodgates open."

"Fifteen," Gray said and pulled Beth into his lap. "It's okay, baby."

"You know, I was feeling a little guilty with the way I went about getting grandbabies, but without me putting a fire under your butts, you wouldn't have Gray, and while I think Deanna and Merrick would have figured it out, I'm not unhappy that we are expanding our family."

Merrick chuckled. "Trenton said you were feeling guilty. What are you going to do about him?"

"Nothing right now. I'm unhappy with him." She reached over and swiped a tear from Beth's cheek. "You're right, he was Mr. Van der Mean."

Beth shook her head.

"No, Mom. I was wrong. He's been nothing but good to you. He's a good man."

Elsa sighed. "He once told me he was a good man who had done some bad things. This was a bad thing."

Deanna got up and started clearing the table.

Gray slid out from under Beth and joined her. That left the three of them to talk.

"When is your surgery?"

"Next week."

Beth gasped. "And you weren't going to tell us." Her voice nearly raised the roof.

"Stop already. I've learned my lesson. I thought I was saving you from worrying."

Beth covered Elsa's hand with hers. "We're your kids. We'll always worry. Besides, this will be excellent practice for when our little ones are born."

"Surgery is Monday. I could be in the hospital for up to three days. Then I'll start hormone therapy." She saw the concern in both her children's eyes. "HER2 positive breast cancer is not hereditary. They believe it's caused by the environment or lifestyle, but you should be vigilant, anyway." She grabbed both of her children's hands and squeezed. "Don't worry, I'll be all right."

"Is Trenton taking you?"

She had no idea anymore.

"No, I hoped that one of you could drive me. It would seem that I've chased my ride away."

"We'll both take you," Merrick said. "But, Mom, you should talk to him. I'm sure he'll forgive you."

That rubbed her the wrong way, but she didn't want to get into it with her kids, so she ignored Merrick's response.

"How about that pie?" Deanna asked.

She brought the pie and plates while Gray got the ice cream. The rest of the evening, they talked about the babies and how much fun next Christmas would be when they all gathered around the Christmas tree.

Elsa got a little melancholy. Not because she'd told the kids. Not because they were upset at her for keeping it close to her vest. She was sad because cherry pie was Trenton and her ritual. He knew she loved it and made sure she had an endless supply.

She knew she needed to forgive him, but could she?

CHAPTER TWENTY

The music played through the jukebox sitting in the bar's corner. A soft ballad about loving someone for better or worse filled the air along with the smell of wood oil and hops.

At the bar sat Doc. In front of him was Cannon, and between them was a napkin where they played Tic Tac Toe.

"Do you ever pay for your beer?" he asked as he took the seat next to Cannon.

"It's a rarity," the bartender said. "What'll you have?"

Trenton pointed to Doc's half-full mug.

"I'll have what he's having."

Doc turned to face him.

"If this is going to be a mentoring session, my beer is on you."

He hated to admit it, but he probably needed the old man's wisdom.

"Put his beer on my tab," Trenton said.

Cannon shredded the napkin with the x's and o's. "Saved me from another loss."

Trenton was pretty sure Cannon let Doc win. The two were close. Almost like father and son. That made him think of his own father. They say the apple doesn't fall far from the tree, and in Cannon's case, that didn't seem to be true. He was a stand-up guy who took responsibility for his life and choices. Word had it that Ben, after the death of his wife, had become the town drunk. He was glad to see that the man had straightened himself up. Maisey had something to do with that. It seemed as if there was a woman behind every success story in this town.

Bea Bennett had been the heart of the town. Since her passing, others had stepped in to take over. Funny how it took an entire village to make up for the one woman.

"What happened to Bea?" Trenton said out loud to anyone who'd answer.

Cannon set his beer in front of him and filled Doc's mug.

"It's been several years now since she passed,"

Doc said. "Congestive heart failure. That woman was the thread that held it all together. Even when she passed, she made sure we didn't fall apart."

He listened as Cannon and Doc explained about the pink letters. A part of him was sad that he hadn't been a recipient.

"So, Bea basically handed you your wife."

Cannon nodded. "And she brought Bowie his wife Katie. That girl had never cooked a thing before she came here. Talk about someone who wasn't giving up."

He explained how Katie had Brandy's heart and how she'd come here to find herself, and in turn found life.

"And the band?" he asked.

"Samantha lived here as a kid, and when her life of fame and fortune had worn her thin, she came back to her happy place," Cannon said.

So much had happened in the town since he'd last been here. How had he abandoned the one place that had always brought him joy? Maybe comparing it to his life was too painful. Once he buried the litmus test for happiness, his life didn't seem so bad. He could justify his discontent because he had things like money and mansions and cars. But what he'd learned over the years was that no amount of money could make him feel whole. Elsa did that.

"I may have messed things up royally."

"This is where the conversation leaves my lane. I'll let you two talk while I take inventory." Cannon moved like a man running for his life.

Doc took a gulp of his beer and wiped the foam from his mustache with the back of his hand.

"You want to tell me what happened, son?"

Trenton remembered a similar conversation with his father. Only that conversation was him telling his dad he'd made a big mistake marrying his ex-wife. His father's advice: you made your bed, now you have to sleep in it.

"I forced Elsa's hand when it came to telling her kids."

Doc nodded slowly, while curling the corner of his mustache.

"And?"

"She booted me out of her house."

He nodded again and sat for several seconds.

"Why did you tell the kids?"

He shook his head. "I didn't tell them, but I caused a situation in which she had to spill the beans."

It would appear that he'd stunned the man who had advice for everyone and every situation into silence.

"Now listen here, son." He laid his hand on the

table and looked at Trenton thoughtfully. "What you did wasn't right." He held up a finger. "However, what she did wasn't the wisest move either. Were your motives good?"

He nodded. "Yes. Elsa will need a support system and her family should be a part of that."

"I thought you were crazy about her."

"I am." Trenton hung his head and sighed. He was wild about the woman.

"And yet, you sacrificed everything."

"In hindsight, maybe I should have said nothing. But it felt right and I'll stick to my decision. Her kids needed to know."

"I've got some experience with this." Doc shifted in his chair like he was getting ready for a long talk.

"I bet you do." Doc Parker seemed to have experienced just about everything. That he was so old and lived through several eras had a lot to do with it. Trenton only hoped that someday, he'd be as wise and able to offer counsel to Mason.

"Do you remember my Phyllis?"

A smile came to Trenton's face as he recalled Doc's wife and how she handed out penny candy at the store. You didn't have to come in for any reason. Phyllis always had a smile and a peppermint for everyone.

"I remember her. I'm sorry for your loss."

"It was a damn shame, but for lots of reasons. I didn't talk to my daughter Charlie for nearly ten years. It wasn't that I didn't want to talk to her, it was that she didn't want to speak to me. I'd withheld information about her mother—important health information, and Charlie blamed me for her death."

"Wow." He couldn't imagine that happening.

"Of course, I didn't kill Phyllis. I loved that woman more than life itself. The point is her kids needed the information. If I had to do it all over again, I would have told Charlie that her mom wasn't well, but like most women, Phyllis was stubborn. She didn't want Charlie to worry."

"Sounds familiar."

"I'll never understand women. They have this maternal gene that doesn't die until they do." He chuckled. "In Bea's case, it kept living through her letters. I keep thinking another is going to show up one day soon. I'm not sure what's left of Bea in town. She gave away the bed and breakfast, the bakery, her daughter's organs. I have no idea if there's anything else, but if there is, I'm positive someone will come calling for it. No matter what, the women I know would do anything to make sure their children avoid grief, but withholding information can cause it. My Phyllis had atherosclerosis. It's a hardening of the arteries. I'm sure it came from a lifetime of eating fried foods and sneaking into the candy jar."

"Maybe you should have this conversation with Elsa. She needs to know what was at stake."

Doc tipped back his beer and gulped it dry. "I imagine she's home thinking about it now." He slid off the chair and moved toward the door. "Thanks for the beer, and don't forget, I'm a good tipper."

Trenton chuckled. "I bet you are."

As Doc walked out, a man walked in. He came straight to the bar and sat in Doc's vacated chair.

"How's it going?" he said. "I'm Alex Cruz." He offered Trenton his hand.

"Nice to meet you. I'm Trenton Van der Veen."

Alex chuckled. "Oh, I know who you are."

Trenton picked up his beer and sipped. "My reputation precedes me."

"Oh, I only know you from the Mason and Jewel situation. You're the one who got her the show back, right?" He cleared his throat. "I'm in show business and that kind of news travels fast."

Could that be true? Could one person in town have heard something good before the bad?

"All news in a small town travels faster than the speed of light."

Alex patted him on the back. "What you did was a solid thing to do."

He was happy to have had the opportunity. All he had to hear was Jewel's closing of the episode, and that sealed the deal. She and his son were meant to be together.

"What brings you to the bar?"

"Mercy kicked me out. She and Maddy are having a girl's night, painting toenails and watching *My Little Pony* cartoons. It's probably the last night they'll have alone together."

Trenton cocked his head. "Everything okay?" While he knew he'd be spending his time alone for the foreseeable future, Alex was young, which meant so was his wife. It didn't make sense.

"Oh yes, we're expecting our first child."

With narrowed eyes, Trenton clarified. "Who's Maddy then?" He hoped it wasn't one of those thripple or thrupple couples. It was hard enough to keep up with one woman. Lord knew two would put him in the grave.

Alex made a silly face.

"I forgot, you're not from these parts."

Trenton smiled. "Oh, I am, but it's been decades."

"I'm Alex, as I said. I'm the drummer for Indigo. Mercy is a transplant to Aspen Cove as well. Maddy is my child." He shook his head. "Don't let Mercy hear me say that. She might not have given birth to Maddy, but she's staking claim."

"When is she due?"

"Any time now." He patted the phone he sat on the bar top. "I'm ready."

"That's what you think, but I'll tell you, there's nothing like having your child placed in your arms for the first time." Trenton smiled at the memory of looking down at Mason and seeing so much of himself in the tiny little boy. "But you already know that."

Alex's expression dimmed.

"I didn't meet Maddy until she was five. I didn't know she existed. Her mom was a..." he leaned in, "...groupie," he whispered.

"Ah, okay. Well then, you're in for a surprise."

"I can't wait. What about you? Why are you sitting alone in the bar?"

Trenton looked toward the door.

"Doc just left."

"Ah, therapy session. I've had a few of those myself."

Trenton reached back for his wallet and pulled it from his pocket.

"I should head out." He laid two twenties on the counter. "That should cover mine, Doc's, and yours. Congrats on the baby."

Alex smiled. "Where are you headed?"

He hadn't thought much about it. He couldn't go back to Elsa's, and he didn't feel comfortable in the flat above The Corner Store. The only place left to go was home.

"I think I'm headed back to Denver for a bit." He turned and headed for the door.

"Are you coming back?" Alex asked.

Now that was the question of the day, and he couldn't answer it.

CHAPTER TWENTY-ONE

Elsa sat in her chair sipping her tea, watching the door and hoping Trenton would come back. She was too stubborn to call and ask him to come home, but that's what she wanted, or so she thought.

At this point, she wasn't certain about anything. Her emotions were in a twist, and she couldn't think straight.

She was torn between right and wrong and still confused about on which side of the fence Trenton stood. The affronted part of her was angry that he'd manipulated the situation. The prideful side of her was hurt because he knew she wanted to be the one to choose. Yes, she was a strong and stubborn woman. Sure, she was used to having her way, and maybe that played into this somewhat.

"Who are you kidding?" she asked out loud. "Your stubborn pride got the best of you."

They say hindsight is 20/20, and that's true. Too bad things can't be played out first and then re-wound, so she could do it all over again with insight.

"Your babies are all grown up and having babies." She shook her head. Why she didn't think they could handle the news, she didn't know.

They sat there stoic and asked the right questions. Beth got a little teary-eyed, but that was understandable. She was a walking hormone factory. As usual, Merrick was his thorough self. He talked to her like he was taking down a crime report. It was a crime really because Elsa had nice breasts, and they were still mostly where they belonged.

Just boobs. Not worth the fight. She opted to not have reconstruction. She'd be happy with the outcome, regardless.

"Beth was so much more in control than I was when Mama told me."

Elsa remembered that day clearly. She bawled for days, but maybe it was because there was little hope for Mama by the time she addressed it. She was the type of woman who wouldn't give something she wasn't interested in any energy. She could hear her mama's voice. "What I don't know can't hurt me." That was the biggest pile of bull dung ever. What she refused to acknowledge took her out.

She wasn't like her mama. She knew something was wrong and made sure someone listened. That was half the problem. Often doctors were so over-whelmed that they didn't take the time to truly hear their patients.

Then there was the group of doctors, who she liked to call old school because they were probably practicing back when they gave women hysterec-tomies to calm down their hysteria. What was wrong with people? The only thing those women needed was a bottle of wine and a girlfriend to talk it out with.

A soft knock at the door brought her out of her thoughts. Her heart rate picked up its pace. If she opened the door and found Trenton, what would she do?

The knock sounded louder this time, and she rose from her chair and walked to the door. Her hand gripped the knob, and she yanked it open to find Beth on her doorstep.

Though she was happy to see her daughter, she was disappointed it wasn't Trenton. He said he wouldn't leave her, but he did. Then again, she'd or-dered him to.

"What are you doing here?"

Beth walked inside and straight to the kitchen. Since she'd organized it for Elsa, she knew exactly where to find the herbal tea.

"I came to give you that wooden spoon whoopin' you deserve. How could you?"

After an exaggerated sigh, Elsa got her teacup and took a seat at the table.

"I was trying to protect you?"

"Were you? Or were you trying to protect yourself? How could you tell Trenton and not tell your own flesh and blood?"

Elsa considered that for a moment.

"First, I wouldn't have told him, but he took me to the appointment and was here when I got the news. It was hard to hide my surprise."

"The diagnosis surprised you?"

Beth was pinning her in a corner. "No, I knew I had it." She rubbed her stomach. "It was a gut feeling. I saw my doctor in Denver and he told me not to worry about it, but I couldn't stop myself. I tried to let it go but then I felt the lump again and went to see Doc Parker."

"Oh, my God. How many people in town know you have cancer?"

Elsa held up her hands and started counting with her fingers, "Including me, I'd say about ten if Sage and Agatha know."

Her daughter plopped a tea bag in her cup and filled it from the insta-hot tap.

"That's eight more than Merrick and me. Don't

we deserve to know what's going on with our mother?"

The guilt Beth piled on was nearly unbearable. She felt bad for her grandson because his mother would never relent.

"I just didn't—"

Beth held up her hand. "You didn't want to stress us. Are you kidding? You're our only parent."

Elsa shook her head.

"That's not true. I didn't have you both from some divine intervention. You have fathers."

Beth grunted. "You can't really call a sperm donor a father. The word itself brings images of family dinners and ballgames. We had none of that."

"Maybe I was to blame for that." She looked into the living room at the couch where she and Trenton had sat, cataloguing the collection. "I seem to send men running."

"You can't count my father because he is an idiot. I don't know about Merrick's, but he sounded like one, too. I'd say you have poor taste in men." Beth sat at the table next to her mom. "But you'd upped your game. Trenton was nice, and you kicked him out of the house."

"He betrayed me."

"Did he, Mom? I mean, really? I think he helped you. Stress eats at people and makes them sicker. Imagine trying to cover up one lie with another." She shook her head. "Honestly, I should wash your mouth out with soap."

Elsa wagged her finger in the air. "I only did that to you once. Five-year-old girls shouldn't be dropping the F-bomb like it was nothing."

Beth rolled her eyes.

"I learned it from you."

Elsa gasped. "I never."

"Oh, you did. You used to tell me you were speaking French." She shrugged. "I wanted to be bilingual too."

Elsa took a drink of her tea. It was peppermint and settled her stomach. It wasn't the dinner that gave her indigestion but the conversation.

"You mastered French by the time you were sixteen."

Beth smiled. "I had colorful friends."

"Despite your stubbornness, you were a good kid, and I was lucky to have you."

Beth placed her hand over her mother's. "I come by it naturally."

"And so will your son." Merrick had divulged the name of their baby, but Gray and Beth hadn't. "What will you call him?"

The light twinkled in Beth's eyes. "He's Gray's son. So that's what he'll be called."

"Grayson." Elsa hummed. "I like it."

"I wanted to name him Motley after Mötley

Crüe, but Gray said no. I suppose he's right. We've got Ozzy Pawsborn, Kitty Van Halen, and Gums and Roses. We can't let our son think he's just one of the pets."

Elsa laughed. "Not a chance of that. Your animals don't know they're pets. I'm fairly certain each of them thinks you're a pet and they own you."

"They do."

Beth had always been a sucker for the underdog. How she ended up with Gray, she didn't know. Well, she did, but that was a story she'd never tell her grandson. She was sure Beth and Gray would stick with the love at first sight story they told everyone else.

"What are you going to do about Trenton? You know, he was only looking out for us. That's something our own fathers never did."

That statement made Elsa's heart hurt. The two men she had children with and tried to keep weren't worthy of her kids, and the one that was, she kicked out.

"I'm going to give it a day. We both need some time to think about all of it. Honestly, I shanghaied Trenton into being with me. One minute he was buying Chinese food, and the next, I was asking him to stay."

She had cried in his arms. She'd let no one see her that vulnerable, and yet he had.

"He wouldn't have stayed if he didn't want to. The one thing I've heard about Trenton was that he never did anything he didn't want to."

"A little time away might give him perspective." She pointed to herself. "Who wants this? I'm middle-aged, and I have cancer."

Beth clucked her tongue.

"He wants that, or he wouldn't have been there. I've never seen you so happy. He made you happy."

She nodded.

"He did, but I can't saddle him with my problems."

"Geez!" Beth hit the table hard enough to make the cups jump. "Stop protecting everyone from yourself. He's an adult. He gets to decide. While I'm certain you can run the universe with one eye closed, you don't have to. People are entitled to make decisions. Only they can say if you're a bad one. Stop being that person who thinks they are in control of everyone and everything. You're not. You never have been. We just let you think that."

"Beth Buchanan, don't you talk to your mother like that. Do I need to get the wooden spoon out?"

"If you take it out, you're first." Beth rose and brought her cup to the sink. "I just came back to make sure you were okay."

She wanted to smile and nod, but she was tired of

being the rock for everyone. The tears spilled down her cheeks.

"No, I'm not."

"I'm here." Beth wrapped her arms around Elsa and held her so close that she could feel her grandson kick.

That made her smile.

"Feels like you're both here." She laid her cheek on Beth's belly until she felt another nudge. "I'm glad because I'm not as strong as everyone thinks."

Beth stood back and looked at her mother.

"Let us be strong for you."

"I'll try." She rose and walked her to the door.

"Let Trenton back in. His motives were good. Sometimes people do the wrong things for the right reasons."

Elsa breathed deeply. She knew her daughter was right, but she'd still give him a little time. He was like that song about setting a bird free. All that was left to do was wait and see if he'd come back to her.

CHAPTER TWENTY-TWO

Trenton wasn't happy walking back into the office. This wasn't the plan. He was supposed to be waking up next to Elsa, but she'd kicked him out. On the three-hour trip back to Denver, he was tempted to turn around several times and rush back to her house, but she was clear on her desires. She wanted him gone.

He didn't know if she wanted him gone for good or temporarily.

He marched past his secretary and into his office to find his desk occupied.

"What the hell are you doing here?" Trenton asked.

Danny Archuleta stared at him like he'd lost his

mind and maybe he had. It took a minute to realize he'd replaced himself.

"Sir, you told me to take over and gave me the keys to your office."

Danny had been with the firm for over ten years and was the best one for the job.

Trenton waved his hand in the air.

"You're right. You're right." He felt silly and so out of place. This was the second place he'd caught himself and others by surprise. When he arrived the night before, he nearly gave his housekeeper a heart attack when he walked inside his downtown penthouse. For an elderly woman, she jumped several inches. It was when she clutched her chest and staggered back that he got worried. He was certain he'd killed the poor woman.

"Would you like your office back?"

Trenton looked around. It all looked the same—mostly. The only change was that it looked warmer with Danny's family photos decorating his desk and his shelves.

"No, I just wanted to stop by and see how you were doing?" he lied. What he was doing was trying to find a moment of calm by inserting himself back into his old life. But his old life had already moved on.

"I'm good. No one has tossed me out an open window yet."

Trenton laughed. "We installed the ones that only open six inches for just that reason."

"Smart." Danny sat in the big chair and waited. "Did you want to talk about anything in particular?" He looked at his watch. "I've got a meeting with the board in five, but I can delay it if you need something."

His chest felt heavy. He'd been kicked out of Elsa's, and now he was getting kicked out of his office. Danny was doing it in a more diplomatic way than she did, but it felt the same.

"No, I've got things to do. I was just in the neighborhood and thought I'd stop by."

The necktie he wore today seemed to tighten. With a tug, he loosened it. It was the same tie he'd been wearing when he met Elsa. She called it his power tie and told him not to wear it to dinner.

He'd really blown it. From the start, Elsa showed him who she was. She was a woman used to running her life because she couldn't count on a man and, once again, he'd proven her right. She'd asked him for his confidentiality regarding her illness and he blew it because he thought he was right. Part of him didn't regret that decision because her kids needed to know, but he should have gently persuaded her to come clean rather than confront her in front of them.

Danny rose. "I'll walk you out."

Trenton wanted to laugh. This had been his domain for decades, and he was the one being escorted out. He was no longer needed there.

"You go to your meeting. I know my way to the door." He patted the man on the back. "You'll do great."

Danny smiled. "I'll make you proud."

"You already have."

Those were the words he owed his son.

As he rode the elevator to the garage, he dialed Mason.

"Dad, what's up?"

"Nothing. I just wanted to talk to you and tell you I'm proud of you."

There was a length of silence that almost seemed uncomfortable.

"Are you sure you're okay?"

"I'm fine, son." He wasn't fine, but he would not whine to his son. He was always of the belief that if you made your bed, you had to sleep in it. He'd created this problem. So he'd fix it.

"Where are you?"

"I'm in Denver."

"You're what? I thought you were staying here for a while?"

He was a leopard that hadn't really changed his spots. He'd returned to find the comfort in his old life only to find that life had moved on without him. No one was irreplaceable, even Trenton Van der Veen.

"Just taking care of a few things. I needed clothes and some personal belongings."

His son cleared his throat.

"That moving company you sent when you turned my world upside down did a good job for me. You should have them pack you up."

Was he ready to make that kind of commitment?

He exited the elevator and went to his car, making his way back to his penthouse.

"I'm really sorry about that. I was making a point."

"You definitely made it." Mason didn't sound angry, though he had a right to be. "And while I was furious back then, I'm grateful now."

Trenton knew it could have turned out far different. "I'm glad it worked out. My empathy gene, my patience gene, and my humanity gene had been shut off for a while. I'm working on that."

"I know you are. And Dad? I'm proud of you too."

His heart felt like a fist was squeezing it. How long had it been since anyone had told him that? He'd always sought his father's approval, but never seemed to make the old man happy. His older siblings had bailed on the family business years before, which should have told him then that making their father proud was impossible. People say you do what you know, and he had. He'd treated Mason the way he was treated, but he could do better, and he would.

"How are things with Elsa?"

That was the million-dollar question.

"We're..." What could he say? He didn't want to lie, but he didn't want to tell his son he'd failed at another relationship. "Oh hell, she's mad at me."

"Seems to be a Van der Veen gift. We irritate the ones we love. You are falling for her, right?"

"I've already fallen. Seems silly looking from the outside in, but she's..."

"Everything that Mom's not?"

He stayed silent. One of his rules was he'd never make disparaging remarks about his son's mother in front of him.

"I know who Mom is. I'm not looking at her through rose-colored glasses. You deserve to be with someone who appreciates you for who you are as a man."

He pulled into the parking garage of his downtown penthouse and sat there to finish the conversation.

"I'm not sure that I have much to offer. Maybe I'm too stuck in my ways."

Mason laughed. "Dad, you just morphed into someone I don't know—someone I'd like to know. I'm fairly certain if you were stuck, you wouldn't have been able to make that transition so easily. You'll figure it out. The one thing I know about you is that you're not a quitter."

"You're right."

Elsa wasn't a quitter either, and he'd be damned if he'd let her quit on him.

"When will you be back?"

"In time for dinner."

Mason seemed to muffle the phone and after a moment of talking to someone, he said, "Barbecue at our place at six."

"I'll be there. Should I bring something?"

"Just yourself."

They ended the call and Trenton felt more pep in his step since he'd arrived the night before. Now he was a man with a mission, and that was to win back Elsa's trust.

He took the elevator to the top floor. As soon as he entered his foyer, he called out to his housekeeper, but she didn't respond. His heart ticked up a beat as he knew she was there. She lived there and her car was in the garage.

As he moved across the vast space, he found her in the kitchen. Sitting at the table were her son Tyler and her daughter-in-law, who were in tears. He met them a time or two when they came to visit their mom.

"Sir," Mary began. "I'm so sorry to take up your

space." She shooed her son and daughter-in-law from the table. "Let's talk later."

Tyler had a sullen, defeated look on his face. It was a look no man wanted to adopt and only came when things were terrible.

"Sit," Trenton said and pointed them back to the table. "Is there something I can help with?"

Tyler said nothing, but his wife burst into tears.

"We got behind on the rent, and they're kicking us out."

Though Trenton wanted to collect a few things and be on his way, he took a seat.

"Are you employed?"

Tyler took a deep breath and nodded.

"Yes, sir. I've been with the same company for ten years, but my rent keeps rising faster than my paycheck and with one in college and the other in high school, things aren't getting any cheaper."

While Trenton would like to say he knew what they meant, he couldn't. He'd never lived a day in his life having to worry about where the rent would come from. He never had to choose between buying a chicken or toilet paper. From their expressions, things were dire.

"I'm sorry to hear that. Rents are out of control, but so are house prices." This last year had netted him more money than he knew what to do with. "And you came here to see if your mom could help?"

Mary burst out into tears. "No, they came to tell me they are going to move out of state to Wyoming where it's cheaper."

He'd never seen his housekeeper cry, and he didn't like it.

He rose from his seat. "Give me a minute to think." He pointed to the fancy coffee machine that took a barista to operate it. "Have a latte and I'll be back in a few. I need to pack up a few things."

He felt bad that they would lose their home. As he walked through his place, it didn't feel like home. Elsa's tiny little house was the only place that felt like home. He even preferred the flat above The Corner Store to this. While the penthouse could be a wonderful home, it reflected who he was: an empty space without warmth.

Right then, he knew how to fix two problems. He would always run back to what he knew until he cut the ties with what he had.

He opened his closet and took out his favorite suit, a couple of cashmere sweaters, and every pair of jeans he owned. He tossed everything into a suitcase and dragged it to the living room.

There, he looked around and felt the same thing. There was nothing he wanted. He glanced at his bookshelf. Nothing but his first edition copies. He scooped those up and set them on the entry table.

When he walked into the kitchen, he found the

family holding hands and saying a prayer. He'd never been the answer to someone's prayer, but maybe he could be now. He waited for them to finish.

"Tyler, I've got the deal of the century for you."

Tyler looked up at him.

"What's that, sir?"

"What do you think of this place?"

Tyler's eyes grew as big as baseballs.

"It's..."

Trenton didn't have time to iron out the details. He wanted to get back to Aspen Cove. "It's yours."

Tyler shook his head like a dog trying to dislodge something from its ear.

"I'm sorry. What did you say?"

"I'm going to be gone for a very long time and this house needs to be turned into a home. It's a sad, cold place that could use the warmth of a loving family. Your mom has served me for years, and I'm sure I was a pain in the caboose."

Mary nodded.

"Call it a bonus."

"But you could sell it," Tyler said.

"I could, but who would that help? I've got more money than Midas and you need a place to live."

Mary rose and placed her hand on his forehead. "Are you sick?"

Trenton laughed. "Nope, I'm feeling better than I've ever felt before." The penthouse had always been his. His ex-wife had the mansion in Cherry Hill, and he stayed here. They really had been married in name only. "Look around and see if it's someplace you'd like to own. I'll sell it to you for a dollar."

"Wait," Tyler said. "You're going to sell me a place for a buck? That's like me stealing it from you. It's got to be worth—"

"One point two million." He looked at Mary. "Your mom gets to stay, and if you ever sell, she gets half." He leaned over and kissed Mary's cheek. "I'll be depositing your severance pay in your account tonight." He'd make sure she was set up for life.

"What happened to you?" she asked.

He smiled. "I fell in love."

CHAPTER TWENTY-THREE

Elsa watched as Trenton got out of his car. She rushed to the mirror and tried to fluff her hair, but only knocked herself upside the head with her cast.

By the time she got it removed, she'd look like a battered woman, and she'd hate the color pink. Really, she should have gotten a black one since it went with everything.

She leaned against the wall and waited for the knock to come, but it didn't. When she peeked out the window, Trenton was nowhere in sight. He hadn't come to see her after all. He was visiting his son.

Feeling frustrated, she grabbed her purse from the table and walked out the door.

"Elsa Buchanan waits for no man."

Since driving with one hand was unsafe, she walked to the diner. Maisey wasn't there, but Louise was and she hollered, "Sit where you want, love. I'll be right with you."

Elsa glanced around the diner. Eating alone was never fun. She skimmed the patrons and found Lloyd a few tables over, sitting with his back to the door.

She snuck up on him and stood at his side. He was looking through some kind of rancher catalogue.

"Mind if I join you?"

He startled, but smiled when he saw her and pointed to the chair next to him.

"Have a seat." He glanced around the diner. "I thought you'd be here with Trenton."

She took a seat, inhaled deeply, and let out an exasperated breath.

"I thought so too." The truth was, she thought she'd be in her house with Trenton. If she had the courage to apologize, then things would go back to normal. But *I'm sorry* wasn't a part of her normal vocabulary. While she believed a person should apologize if they were in the wrong, this wasn't a clear-cut situation. "We've had a bit of a falling out."

Lloyd's brows shot up.

"Really?" He frowned. "You want to talk about it?"

She shrugged. "Not really. All I want is a patty melt, a chocolate shake, and a piece of cherry pie."

He reached into his pocket and pulled out a roll of Tums. "You'll want these too."

She took them from his hand. "I won't want them, but I'll need them."

Louise worked her way around the diner until she got to them.

"You eatin', love?"

Elsa told her what she wanted.

"You either have a hollow leg or a heartbreak. I'll get right on it." She pivoted and dashed away.

Elsa imagined she got her quickness from having so many kids. If the rumors were true, she had eight of them.

"Does she really have eight kids? How do these big families survive?"

Lloyd laughed. "My wife and I had six."

She let out a slow whistle. "That's a lot, but with you, I get it. You have a ranch and ranch families, like farm families, are bigger. You need hands to help."

He picked up a fry and dragged it through the ketchup. "After having five girls and only one boy, I needed my shotgun and extra shells. I know what boys are about." He ate the fry and looked at her. "What about you? What happened to the men in your life?"

"Do you have a few hours?" she joked.

"I ain't going nowhere."

"That's what they all say." Louise brought over

her shake and disappeared as fast as she'd arrived. "It appears I'm like Julia Roberts in Pretty Woman. I'm a bum magnet. I'm not talking about lazy, no income bums. I'm talking about men who refuse to step up and take responsibility."

"What did Trenton do to you?" He gripped his knife so hard she watched his knuckles blanch white.

"Nothing." If she was going to swallow her pride, this was as good a time as any. It was the rewind she hoped for, but practice made perfect.

"Now, come on. You can't say you had a falling out and there be nothing to it."

She sucked the thick shake through the straw and hummed at the rich chocolate taste.

"Okay, it's going to spread like wildfire anyway, so I might as well just say it." She tapped her nails on the table and waited for the words to force them-selves out, but they stayed locked up inside. That was half of her problem. After two betrayals, she was like a deodorant commercial. She let no one see her sweat. Right then, she felt like a gazelle standing in front of a lion. She and Lloyd weren't a thing, and he couldn't hurt her, but everyone knew that the weaker animal always got slaughtered. That was why she hid behind her ferocious facade. The problem was that everyone was seeing behind it, and she couldn't keep up the act any longer.

"Tell me." His brows furrowed so deeply, they created fissures in the center of his forehead.

"I have cancer."

Lloyd dropped his fork and stared at her.

"You what?"

"I have breast cancer and I'm having surgery on Monday."

Lloyd's skin turned pale.

He reached into his pocket and pulled out a crumpled twenty.

"I'm sorry, but I've got to go." He pushed his chair back with such force that it toppled over.

He gave her a weak smile and nearly tore up the black and white checked flooring, trying to get away.

"Where did he rush off to?" Louise asked.

She placed Elsa's patty melt on the table.

"I scared him away."

Louise looked around and took his seat. "There's only two things that I know will send a man running like that. They're 'I'm pregnant' or 'I've got the crabs,' and seeing as you're not squirming in your seat, I'll give you my congratulations."

"Pregnant?" she said, a little too loud. A soft murmuring spread through the diner. "That's not it."

Louise leaned toward her and whispered, "Doc can take care of the other for you then."

"Geez Louise, I don't have crabs. I've got cancer."

Louise sat back and stared at her.

"I'd rather you were pregnant, had the crabs, and a case of the clap rather than cancer."

It wasn't funny, but she couldn't stop laughing.

"You and me both." She considered having a venereal disease and recanted. "I'd rather not deal with the last one. That sounds awful. Al Capone died from it."

"All the mafia stuff, guns and murder and mayhem, and that's the thing that takes him out. Crazy world." She shook her head. "But let's talk about you. What can I do?"

"Tell me why men always leave?"

She leaned back in the chair.

"In Lloyd's case, I imagine he's afraid you'll die on him like his wife. The others were simply stupid. Look at you. You're beautiful and smart and obviously got your stuff together."

"But they always leave."

"Do they, or do you push them away before they have a chance to leave?" The door opened and Doc and Agatha walked inside. Doc nodded toward her and continued to his booth on the right side of the restaurant. Even if the diner was full, no one ever sat there. It was like an unwritten rule that it belonged to him.

She watched the two of them together and smiled. Doc waited for Agatha to sit before he took his own seat. He handed her a menu before he got one for himself. He had impeccable manners. Old-fashioned, stand-out manners like Trenton.

Louise's words played on repeat. *Do you push them away before they have a chance to leave?*

That was exactly what she did. She was pissed at Trenton, but instead of acting like the grown up she was, she'd let her inner five-year-old out and let her take over.

Yep, she'd made a big mistake and now she had to fix it. They would have to talk, but a conversation like that needed sustenance and pie. She sat there for the next hour and ate her patty melt, fries, and a jumbo piece of pie while she planned her words.

All she could really come up with was, "I'm sorry. I'm such an idiot." That should work. It was short and to the point.

She paid her bill and walked back home, but when she arrived, Trenton's car was gone, and her heart sank to her heels.

Her insides twisted, her shoulders stiffened, and her skin prickled as she walked over and knocked on the door.

Mason opened it.

"Elsa. Are you okay? Do you need something?"

"You father didn't come home last night." It might have been odd to refer to her place as his home, but it felt less homey without him and made her wonder if a person could feel like home, too.

He nodded and smiled. "He went back to Denver."

"Oh, okay." She turned and walked away before he could see the tears run down her cheeks. When he called her name, she pretended not to hear him while rushing to get inside her house.

Reality set in immediately. She had truly chased him away.

CHAPTER TWENTY-FOUR

Trenton parked behind The Corner Store and sat in his car staring at the scarred metal door. How many people had walked through it? He never thought about the impact of a door until fifteen minutes ago when he'd knocked on Elsa's. He knew she was there because her car was in the driveway.

She was still mad at him. That was the only reason for her to not answer the door. He knocked several times and even pleaded against the frame for her to let him in, but no sound came from within.

Now he was back to the efficiency unit above the store where the hum of the equipment below would either drive him nuts or put him to sleep.

Mason and Jewel had offered him their spare room, but he declined. It was hard enough being in the same town with Elsa when she was giving him the cold shoulder. He couldn't imagine being next door.

"When did I turn into this guy?" He opened the door and exited, reaching into the backseat for his suitcase. "You're like a puppy begging for attention."

He yanked his suitcase free and trudged to the door. He jammed the key into the lock and threw open the door.

"When will someone just love me?"

"What's that noise out there?" a gruff voice said from above. "Keep it down. Jeopardy is on."

If he hadn't recognized it as Doc, he would have thought the Almighty was punking him.

"It's just me, Doc. It's Trenton." He backed up and stared to where Doc peeked over the windowsill.

"What are you doing back?"

He shook his head. "Long story. I'll meet you in the bar tomorrow for a beer."

Doc shook his head. "I'll tell Lovey I'll be gone for two. It sounds like you need an ear."

"Yep, I need an ear, and I'll buy the beer."

Doc chuckled. "That's how it works." He disappeared through the window and slammed it shut.

That seemed to be the way of his life these days. It was supposed to be that when one door closed, another opened, but he was being pushed out of everything and away from everyone.

He locked the door behind him and dragged his bag up the flight of stairs to enter what was now his home. He'd fallen a long way from a penthouse apartment in a Denver high-rise. Then again, he was on the second floor of the highest building in town.

Inside was a small bed, a wall that served as the kitchen, and a small bathroom tucked behind the kitchen. There was a chair that sat across from a television. It wasn't the eighty incher he had in the media room of the old house but more like the size of a laptop attached to the wall.

It wasn't opulent. Hell, he wasn't even sure there was cable, but it was home. And until he could figure out a way to get back into Elsa's good graces, it was all he had.

THE NEXT MORNING, Trenton sat in the diner. From the moment he walked inside to now, every eye in the place peeked, glanced, or stared at him. If he glared back, all he got was a frown and a shake of the head.

How long would it take for him to overcome the Van der Mean name? He bought up all the property in Aspen Cove.

He picked up a menu and held it in front of his

face just to get a break from the piercing visual daggers thrown his way.

"Coffee, doll?" Maisey leaned against the red leather-ish bench.

"I'd love coffee." He looked up from the menu. "What's going on?" He turned over the white mug sitting in front of him. "Is there something on my face? Everyone seems to be staring at me."

Maisey filled his cup.

"You know people. If there's a story to be told, they're going to hear it and pass it around."

He imagined in the scuttlebutt around town he was being portrayed as the beast and Elsa, the beauty. And while he wouldn't argue that she was beautiful, he wasn't nearly as bad as people made him out to be.

"I made a mistake."

"I wouldn't call it that exactly. Some people might find that offensive." She pulled her pad from her pocket. "What's it going to be ... stud."

The way she said it, he half expected her to put out a fiery ember with her loafer on the checked tile floor and the occupants in the diner to break out in song and dance. Maybe the motorcycle on display to rev loudly and leave its pedestal hanging above the counter. But this wasn't a version of the movie *Grease*.

"Umm, what about pancakes and sausage?"

Maisey wrote it down and looked at him thoughtfully.

"How old are you?"

He didn't understand the context of her question. Was there an age limit to pancakes? He wasn't asking for a kid's meal.

"Fifty-eight."

She whistled. "You'll be close to eighty."

He blinked several times. "I'm sorry. What?"

"The baby. Can you handle having kids around when you're almost eighty?"

A table in the corner flagged Maisey, and she trotted off before he could get her to clarify. His heart raced. Could it be? He smiled. The only answer was that Mason and Jewel were expecting, and he'd be a grandfather. A jolt of excitement rushed through him. Now he understood the appeal. He hadn't been around many babies, but the thought of being a grandfather excited him. It would give him a kind of do-over. A second chance to get everything he'd done wrong with Mason right with his grandchild.

His mind went to Elsa and how she'd initiated her role as a grandma. When he looked up, several eyes were on him again.

"Yes," he said, pointing to himself. "There's a baby entering my life."

As if they were ashamed for staring, every eye in the place lowered.

231

Maisey came back to his table ten minutes later with a plate filled with cakes and sausage. He lifted his head and smiled.

"I'm going to have a baby in the family?"

She laughed. "That's the rumor."

"I have to call Mason. I hate that the news came through town gossip."

Maisy tore off the check and laid it on the table.

"Town gossip is often quicker than a phone call."

He pulled out his phone to dial his son, but set it on the table. It would be better to get the information in person. Besides, that would give him another opportunity to knock on Elsa's door.

For his entire meal, he grinned like a fool. People always said becoming a grandparent was the best thing. He couldn't even imagine the experience a year ago, but now it opened so many possibilities.

He cleaned his plate and paid his bill and headed toward Mason's house.

When he got there, Elsa's car was in the driveway, just like the night before.

He debated going there first, but he knew once she answered the door, they would have an extended conversation.

Right now, he needed to see Mason.

The door opened before he got to the porch and Mason stood there with a smile on his face.

"Congratulations are in order. I mean, it happened so fast, but no one's getting any younger, right?"

"Exactly. Better to have them while I can still tie my shoes and remember my name." Trenton chuckled. "Where's Jewel? I wanted to see her too."

"Come on in." Mason stepped aside. "You just missed her. She's watching the store today while Beth takes Elsa to an appointment."

His alarm bells went off.

"Why does she need to see the doctor?"

Mason walked into the kitchen and poured himself a cup of coffee.

"You want a cup?"

He shook his head. "No, why is Elsa at the doctor?" He wasn't aware of any appointments, but Elsa told him those things on an as-needed basis. Still, he didn't like that he wasn't the one taking her. He'd promised to be there, and she wasn't allowing him to fulfill his promise.

"Dad, I imagine a woman in her condition and at her age will require special care."

He couldn't argue about her condition. She would need special care while she was going through treatment. Her age was another matter. It wasn't as if she were old. Elsa was in her fifties. That was seven in dog years. She was just a pup. Wasn't fifty the new thirty?

"You're right."

"I can't imagine what she's going through."

Trenton walked into the kitchen and leaned against the counter. "Me either. Cancer is a scary beast."

"Yes. Do you think she'll delay her treatment? I mean, can they even treat her at this point?" He brought his cup to his lips and took a drink.

Trenton cocked his head. He wasn't following. "Why in the hell couldn't she be treated?"

His son looked at him like he'd grown a third eye.

"Dad, pregnancy is risky at her age, but to throw in surgery and drugs... Surely you see that."

Trenton gripped the edge of the counter so tightly, he was certain he'd crack the new granite Jewel had installed. Something was off with this conversation. His body knew it. His internal stress thermometer was ready to explode.

"I'm not following you. What does Jewel's pregnancy have to do with Elsa?"

Mason was mid-sip when he spit out his coffee, sending a shower across the room.

"Jewel? Pregnant?" He shook his head. "Jewel's not pregnant."

"But the baby?"

Mason set his cup on the counter and walked toward Trenton.

"Oh no. I thought you knew. Haven't you talked to Elsa?"

234

He shook his head.

"No, she wasn't there when I knocked."

"Ah, that's why she came here looking for you. When she didn't find you here, she left in tears. Dad ... Elsa is pregnant. Congratulations, Daddy."

"That's impossible ... I mean, it's possible, but how would she know so soon?" The reality of the situation hit him like a brick to the chest. "Oh my God, how is she going to have my baby and surgery?"

Mason looked at him. "That's what I've been trying to get across. You really didn't know?"

"No, we haven't talked."

"I thought it odd that she said you hadn't come home, but then I figured she'd find you. I shouldn't be the one delivering this news. You can't tell her I told you."

"How did you find out?"

He smiled. "Small town. Poppy heard it in the diner, and told Mark, then he told Aiden, who told Marina, who probably told all her clients. I heard when the mailman delivered today."

"I don't know what to say."

"Dad, you can't say anything."

Trenton shook his head.

"Someone's got to say something."

Mason laughed.

"Oh, people are saying lots of things."

"I've got to go." He hugged his son and walked out the door, heading straight toward Copper Creek.

An hour later, he arrived at the office where he'd taken her before. She wasn't there and because of privacy rules, no one would give him information.

He drove around town, but looking for Elsa was like looking for a needle in a haystack. His only option was to return to Aspen Cove. When he did, he climbed out of his car and knocked on her door.

Only silence answered, so he took a seat on the step and vowed to wait until she returned.

Would she tell him herself or would he need to drag the truth out of her?

CHAPTER TWENTY-FIVE

"How fun was that?" Elsa asked.

"Are you talking about the baby shopping or the oncologist appointment?" Beth turned onto Main Street and drove toward her mother's home. "Because I wasn't a fan of that."

Elsa chuckled. What else could she do?

"Both. Up until this morning I was dead set against new boobs, but honestly, I'm going to get them and they'll be right where they were when I was twenty." Originally, she'd opted not to have reconstruction. What was the point? She hadn't had a man in her life in years, so nice boobs weren't a priority. Besides, that meant another surgery, and while she thought she could get away with hiding one, she knew she'd never be able to cover up two. Now that her kids knew, it wasn't necessary to hide anything. "As for the shopping, that was so much fun. I didn't have to go gender neutral."

"True, but I'm pretty sure little Aidy doesn't need a tutu in every color."

Elsa laughed. "You're probably right, but little Grayson probably doesn't need overalls in a rainbow of colors either."

"Oh, yes, he does."

As Beth worked her way through the side streets and turned onto Elsa's, she asked, "What are you going to do about Trenton?"

Elsa turned toward Beth. "I'm going to apologize but I'm not ready yet."

"You better get ready," she said as they neared. "Because he's waiting on your porch."

"Oh, Lord. What is that man doing here?" She pulled down the visor and opened the mirror. "I look a mess."

"Mom ... I don't think he cares."

"You're probably right. I mean, he left and went back to Denver."

Beth pulled into the driveway and killed the engine.

"If he did, he wasn't there for more than a day because he's back to staying above the store."

Elsa whipped out her lipstick and slicked on a layer. She had two rules for when she got old. Never be seen without her hair done and lipstick on, and if her kids found her incapacitated, they were supposed to call 911 and fix her up before anyone got there.

"I'm not used to this relationship stuff. I was never very good at it. What do I do?"

Beth laughed. "Talk to him. It will all work out, and if it doesn't, then at least you have closure."

Elsa watched as he neared the car. She unhooked her seat belt and reached for the handle, but he opened the door first.

"Where have you been?" He offered her his hand, and she took it.

She stared up at him and saw the concern in his eyes, and behind that, she noticed something that looked like hurt.

"We've been shopping for the baby."

The muscles in his jaw ticked, and his cheeks turned the color of an overripe peach.

"Another secret that you're keeping? When will you learn, Elsa?"

She stepped out of the car and stood as tall as she could. There was no way she'd let him intimidate her. Men had been controlling her life or the lack of a life for decades. She wasn't letting another one do the same.

Beth leaned over and smiled. "Play nice, you two. I've got to get home and show Gray everything we bought." Beth pulled out of the driveway, leaving Trenton and her standing there staring at each other.

"If you're going to bully me, you can turn right around and leave." She sidestepped him and walked toward the door.

"Bully you? What do you mean? You're the one withholding information."

"Fine." She stomped her foot and spun around. "I'm getting the boobs."

He stumbled forward.

"What do boobs have to do with this?"

She walked into the house and left the door open so he could follow. Her first stop was the kitchen, where she made them both a tea and then she took a seat at the table.

"If you weren't talking about my boobs, what in the hell are you talking about?"

He sunk into the chair and sighed.

"Elsa." He reached across the table and took both of her hands in his. "I'm talking about our baby."

There was a moment of silence as she let that sink in, but it made little sense.

"Our what?"

"Honey, you don't have to hide from me. I'm thrilled, but I'm worried." His face morphed from stoic to stupid happy. "At my age, I wasn't expecting it but it's a gift. The problem is ... your cancer."

"My cancer is a problem," she said. "But I'm not following you. What does age have to do with cancer?"

He moved his chair so he was sitting right next to her, and placed a hand on her flat belly.

"Can you still have the treatment and be pregnant?"

She sat back so forcefully, the chair almost tipped.

"You think I'm pregnant?" She closed her eyes and tried to imagine where he got that idea, and it dawned on her. The diner. Lloyd. Louise. All the looks of the patrons when she blurted the word pregnant.

She laughed. "Thankfully, I didn't blurt the words 'the clap.'" Her hand settled on his shoulder, where she tried kneading some of the tension out. "Honey, I'm not pregnant."

He cocked his head, and she watched to see if he was disappointed or relieved. He seemed a little of both.

"But everyone in town is talking about it."

She pulled back and sipped her tea. "It's a rumor." She explained the situation.

His laugh started in his stomach and reached his shoulders until he couldn't sit still.

"I was trying to figure out how you knew so quickly. Technology is amazing, but to find out that fast was baffling."

She removed both of their tea bags and set them on a nearby napkin.

"Were you really excited?"

His blue eyes pierced her soul. "Honestly, I was, but it also scared me to death. I didn't imagine that I'd be attending my child's high school graduation when I was rounding eighty. Mostly, I was worried about you. While we haven't been together long, I feel like I know you and you would have put off treatment to see the pregnancy through."

He knew her. She would have done whatever it took to save her baby. No matter what life handed her, her focus had always been on her kids and making sure they had what they needed, and they turned out to be good humans.

"You're right, but guess what?" She clapped her hands. "I'm not pregnant and I don't have a venereal disease."

"I'm relieved." He swiped his forehead with exaggeration. "Now what's this about your boobs?"

She reached out and popped him in the arm with her fist.

"Typical man. It's always the boobs." She was teasing him, but it was kind of true. In her experience, men thought of three things. Sports. Food. Sex. "I've decided to do reconstruction."

He sipped his tea and stayed silent for a long moment. Trenton was a think before he spoke kind of man. She imagined nothing came out of his mouth that he hadn't analyzed repeatedly. She could almost see the gears turning and couldn't wait to hear his response.

"While your breasts are lovely," he glanced at her chest, "they are not what defines you. I like you for who you are. I don't care if you have breasts or not. What's more important is what's behind them ... your heart."

She stared at the man in front of her and wanted to reach up and slap herself upside the head. She'd sent him away. Louise was right, maybe not about the others, but about Trenton. She'd pushed him away.

"I'm sorry I pushed you away."

He leaned forward and rested his hands on her shoulders.

"I understand why you did it. I was wrong. You were right, the story was yours to tell, and I shouldn't have forced your hand."

Her body drifted forward until her lips were inches from his.

"True, but you forced me to do what was right. I'm not sure if you did the right thing for the wrong reasons or the wrong thing for the right reasons. At this point, it doesn't much matter. What matters is that we come to an understanding." She wasn't used to being so honest with someone. It wasn't like she was a liar. She just kept personal stuff private, but she understood how much that hurt her kids and Trenton, and she vowed to not do that again.

"You can tell me anything, Elsa, and I promise to take it to my grave."

She pressed her forehead to his. "Don't talk about graves when I'm getting the breasts of a twenty-year-old in a few months."

"What am I going to do with a twenty-year-old?" He made the same face she was sure she did when she sucked on lemons.

"Just the boobs. The rest is all fifty-something me."

He rubbed his nose against hers. "I love fifty-something you."

She pressed her lips softly against his and said, "I love you, too." When the kiss finished, she pulled back. "It feels like home again."

"You want me to stay?"

She was no longer afraid to ask for the help she knew she'd need.

"Always." She kissed him again, only this time she hoped he felt the promise of forever on her lips. "In case you forgot, we *are* having a baby." She held up one finger and then two. "I mean two. How do you feel about being a grandpa?"

"Are you asking me to marry you?"

She laughed. "No," she said, appalled. "I may be a modern woman, but with love I'm old-fashioned. I want Mr. Darcy, down on one knee."

CHAPTER TWENTY-SIX

Trenton paced the waiting room.

"How long has it been?" he asked anyone who would answer.

"It's only been an hour. The surgeon said it could take a couple," Merrick said.

They all came, but the kids asked him to drive their mom. It wasn't because they didn't want to, but a gift from them to him. They must have seen how much he needed to be with her.

Since their talk that day, life had been blissful. Once they were past this hump, it would continue to be so.

Elsa was exactly who he wanted. She was bossy enough to keep him in line and down to earth enough to keep him humble. She would make him a better man and he would break down all those walls she'd erected to protect her heart.

He went back to pacing until Alex Cruz walked into the room.

"I heard you were here." He went over to his bandmate Gray and shook his hand.

"You came to check on Elsa?"

He shook his head.

"Nope, we were in the mall when Mercy's water broke. Thankfully, Maddy was playing at Louise's house." He grinned like a schoolboy after getting his first feel. "I'm a father." He blushed. "I mean ... again."

The nervous air that filled the room lightened, and congratulations were said. For a minute Trenton let his worry about Elsa ease.

"Boy or girl?"

Alex stood tall. "I've got a son. He's 7 pounds, 12 ounces and 22 inches tall. He looks just like his mother."

Gray slapped him on the back. "Good thing, because if he had your ugly mug, you'd have to pay for him to have a date."

The men chuckled while Beth and Deanna shook their heads.

"If I recall correctly, you've both had panties in the fence problems." She turned her attention to Alex. "What's his name?"

"Maddy wanted to name the baby Rainbow Sherbet, but Mercy and I decided to make sure he didn't have to learn how to fight in kindergarten, so we narrowed it down to Richard or Michael. And since we all know what the shortened version of Richard turns into, we agreed on Michael. It's simple and Mike is a good name too."

The doors across the hall opened, and the surgeon walked out. He went straight to Trenton.

"She's out of surgery and doing well. We'll have her in recovery for a while before we take her to a room. Who wants to see her? I'll allow two of you at a time."

Trenton wanted to rush through the door to be at her side, but he pointed to Merrick and Beth.

"You two go. Your mother will be happy to see you and I'm sure you need to see her as well."

Merrick patted him on the back.

"Thanks for that." He looked at his sister. "We won't take too long."

What was only five minutes seemed like an hour. Once the kids returned, he rushed inside.

Elsa looked beautiful. For a woman who'd just had surgery, it appeared her hair was styled and her lipstick on.

"Honey, how are you?"

She smiled, but it faded. "Groggy and uncomfortable." She pointed toward the bindings that peeked from beneath her gown. "This is a terrible weight loss plan." She gave him a weak smile.

He pulled up a seat and took her hand in his, making sure not to get tied up in her IV tubing or any of the other monitor leads attached to her.

"You look wonderful." He rose and kissed her on the lips. "I don't know how you do it, but you look stunning."

She smiled. "I trained Beth right. There was no way she'd let you come in here and see me looking like I'd just had surgery."

"But baby, you did."

She squeezed his hand. "But no one has to know." She winked and then dozed off to sleep.

THE NEXT MORNING, he showed up with her favorite coffee, several vases of daisies, and a present. He waited outside until it turned eight and visiting hours began.

"Good morning, beautiful." He swept into the room, placing flowers on the table beside her bed.

She sat up, but winced.

"You're in a good mood."

"I'm here with you. That makes everything perfect."

She sank into her pillow and sighed.

"Did you know it's impossible to sleep in a hospital?" She nodded toward her bed table. On it was a copy of *Field and Stream*.

"I've heard." He put the bag he had on the floor and picked up the magazine. "Taking up a new hobby?" This edition was about fly-fishing in Colorado rivers.

"No, that's all they had. I swear, when I get out of here, I'm going to figure out a way to get these people better reading material."

He reached into the bag and pulled out a thermos and poured her a cup of coffee.

"Maybe this will be better."

She took a drink and hummed.

"Oh, my goodness. That's so good." She took another sip. "Why can't they make good coffee here? They brought me some earlier, and it wasn't much better than dirty water."

He leaned back in the chair.

"If the coffee was excellent and the rest was peaceful, nobody would want to leave."

"There is the food." She leaned over to look at the bag. "What else do you have in there? Pancakes and sausage by chance?"

He laughed. "No, but I snuck you a breakfast sandwich and hash browns. Can you have them?"

He took them from the bag and held them in front of her.

She swiped them from his grasp.

In seconds, she was eating like a death row inmate having her last meal.

When she finished, she licked her fingers and wiped her mouth.

"If we were home, I'd say that was foreplay."

He shook his head and pulled out the last thing from the bag and handed it to her.

While she delicately picked at the gift wrap, he poured her more coffee.

When the paper fell away, she gasped.

"Trenton, this is a first edition."

He knew because he'd owned it for over twenty years. It was one of his prized possessions.

Her hands stroked the cover. "It's in nearly perfect shape."

"I take care of the things that are important to me."

Even though she wasn't feeling perfect, there was a playful light in her eyes.

"This is foreplay. A cup of coffee and a first edition of *Pride and Prejudice*. You had me at the coffee." She lifted the book. "But this..."

He kissed her gently.

"I'll take a raincheck."

CHAPTER TWENTY-SEVEN

It had been three weeks since she got out of the hospital, three weeks of Trenton seeing to her every need. The man missed his calling as a home health-care specialist.

"Are you almost ready?"

She looked in the mirror and smiled. Her cast was off, her wounds were healing, and her heart was full.

"Where are we going? I have to know so I can choose something appropriate to wear."

He slid behind her and wrapped his arms around her middle, setting his chin on her shoulder.

"Anything you wear will be perfect." He tugged at the tie on her robe. "You can even wear this. It doesn't matter. You're beautiful the way you are."

She was beginning to believe him. No matter where they were, Trenton only had eyes for her. He was everything she'd dreamed of and more.

"Fine, I'll wear my robe then." She might have been trying to be less secretive and let him in, but she'd never be easy. Easy didn't keep him guessing and she imagined part of what attracted Trenton to her was the surprise.

"Fine," he said. "Let's go. We're going to be late."

"I will not wear a robe." She breezed past him to the closet and shifted things around until she found her lavender sun dress. It wasn't too fancy or too dressed down. Whatever he had in store for her outside of fly-fishing or skydiving, she was certain it would work.

While she'd opened up to him, he'd been secretive lately. Phone calls that ended when she'd entered the room. Secretive discussions in the corners of the diner. Even her kids were in on it. They pretended to come by and see her, but they always managed to drag Trenton outside her hearing range.

Yep, something was up. No one was talking, but she was clever, and after putting it all together, she imagined it had something to do with the historical museum. He'd been pressing her to catalogue the items and boxes were showing up every day. Even a large antique buggy showed up on her grass one day. Trenton quickly had it removed.

"Are you going to tell me about the museum location?" She pulled the dress over her head.

"How did you know?"

"I'm smart that way."

He smiled.

"Yes, you are."

"It doesn't take a rocket scientist. Everyone has been stealing you away from me. The clear giveaway was when Jewel asked if you wanted stone or hardwood floors. It's not as if you're building a house." Her heart tumbled. "You're not, are you?"

It never occurred to her he might be. They hadn't spoken of a future together. She'd just assumed. He said he'd never leave her, but they all did. She erased that thought from her head. Trenton wasn't like the others. He was so much worse and so much better.

"I'm not leaving you. Don't forget, I didn't leave you the last time when you kicked me out."

She rushed to him and threw her arms around his neck.

"I'll never do that again."

He laughed. "I'm pretty sure you'll try, but you can't get rid of me that easily."

She beamed because that was almost as good as a promise of forever.

"Where is the museum going to be?"

"Exactly where we said it would be." He put his arm around her and led her to the door.

"In the schoolhouse? But it's just a pile of wood."

He opened the door and walked her to the car.

"It was, and now it's more." He helped her inside and shut the door.

She couldn't imagine anyone being able to fix the pile of rubble. It was like one of those homestead houses that the land ate up after several hundred years, but this piece of land didn't have a voracious appetite and kind of nibbled at the timber and stone year after year.

"Are you breaking ground today? Does Lloyd know? He's very particular." She felt bad for the man who'd lost his wife. Theirs was one of those love stories that could be told in books. He'd come by to see how she was and apologize, but he never mentioned the museum.

"Lloyd knows and he'll be there. In fact, he was instrumental in the entire process."

Her mind reeled as he backed out of the driveway and took the twenty-minute drive to the edge of the county.

As they approached, she had to blink several times because in place of the old rotting timber was a new building. A square building with a bell on top, just like the pictures she'd found of the old schoolhouse.

She could close her eyes and imagine the teacher

pulling on the bell's string to let the children know school was about to begin.

"How?"

"It's the work of the Cooper brothers." He stopped the car and rushed around to help her out. Her eyes were fixed on the building, and she walked past what appeared to be most of the town.

"You sure like to do it big, don't you?"

He took her hand and held it.

"No, honey. I like to do it right." He walked her to where the bell pull hung. "Do the honors?"

With girlish giddiness, she took hold of the thick rope and pulled down. The rich sound echoed through the trees.

"It's wonderful."

"Do you think you could put together a place where future generations can visit and reflect on their past?"

"I can't wait." Warmth moved through her veins. "I could start now."

He shook his head. "You'll have to wait for a few more minutes. I've got something else for you."

She gripped his arm.

"Trenton, the day is already perfect. How could it get any better?"

In front of the crowd, with her children standing right there, Trenton took a knee.

"Elsa Buchanan, I love you. I think I've loved you

from the moment you told me to leave my red tie at home. I knew I was a goner when you swindled me out of that house." He cleared his throat and pulled a velvet box from his pocket. "'It is a truth universally acknowledged, that a single man in possession of a good fortune must be in want of a wife.'" He opened the box to show a simple band and a small solitaire. Yes, he knew her well. She'd told him early on that she wasn't interested in taking his fortune. Nope, his money didn't matter. All she wanted was his heart. "I'm in want of you. Will you be mine?"

There were collective oohs and ahs, and then silence. Everyone was waiting for her answer. If she'd been Elizabeth, her answer would have been no until Darcy had proven himself, but Trenton had already done that.

He looked at her with eyes that promised her everything, and she knew they told the truth because Trenton Van der Veen had already proven that he was a man of his word.

"Why, Mr. Darcy, my answer is yes."

He slipped the ring on her finger and stood.

"You know what this means, right?"

She giggled. "That I get half of all your first editions?"

He pulled her to him and kissed her. "You're stuck with me forever."

"That doesn't seem very long."

Merrick walked up next to them and grinned.

"Hey, Dad, you want to open the place and give us a look?"

Trenton handed Merrick the keys. "You go ahead. I think I'm going to kiss your mother some more."

ANOTHER PINK ENVELOPE is on its way. Are you ready? Next up is One Hundred Intentions

SNEAK PEEK AT ONE HUNDRED INTENTIONS

Reese Arden had a voice, but unlike other people, her words didn't spill from her lips. Instead, her words spilled onto paper, but no one knew they were hers. She was a two-time New York Times Bestselling Author, but her name wasn't on the covers. She had ghostwritten them for someone else. She did the work, and they got the accolades.

Her whole life, she'd hidden in the background. Some would call her a wallflower. If she spoke, she would have said she was the root of that flower, hidden far beneath the soil, so no one saw her, heard her, or shamed her.

She turned up the radio and belted out a song about love. Too bad people didn't sing their way through life. If that were the case, she'd be an excellent verbal communicator. When she sang, her voice was fluid and flawless, but when she spoke, her stutter chopped up the messages she wanted to convey, and people lost interest in listening. Her speech impediment kept her silent and loveless.

As she drove toward Aspen Cove, there were three things she knew for sure: she couldn't stay silent forever, she needed more than the love her dog Z could give her, and she needed to own her work. Three truths that needed three plans of action. She would be heard, no matter how painful the process would be for others. She'd write a book and slap her name on the cover to see how it did. It was time to own her contribution. The hardest plan to implement would be opening herself up to the idea of love.

She laughed. "Maybe I can f-f-f-find a d-d-deaf man who would l-l-love me. I could l-l-learn sign language."

Z hopped from the back seat and sat on the passenger seat beside her. His head cocked to the side. Like most people who heard her speak, he always had that confused look about him, as if he were trying to decipher what she said. Once he figured out the word "treat" was absent from the sentence, he curled into a ball and sighed.

"I know, b-b-big disappointment." That's what she'd always felt like. She wasn't the kid her parents expected, but the one they got. No one could figure out why she stuttered. There had been no childhood trauma, no medical condition like a stroke or brain injury. All they could say was it was an emotional trigger.

A ball of anxiety got lodged in her throat each time she tried to speak. She glanced at Z, who looked like she'd tossed his favorite ball in the trash.

"You're going to love it in Aspen Cove." She wasn't sure if that was the truth, but she figured it would be more exciting than her apartment in Oklahoma. "We're staying at the lake house. There's w-w-water and b-b-birds to chase." She'd spent some time there as a kid. Her mother and Uncle Frank inherited the property when her grandparents died. No one lived there full time.

"It's cool that Uncle Frank said I could stay." She giggled. "He thinks I'm bringing some friends." She shrugged. "I told him that so he'd stay in Silver Springs. I love the man, but he looks at me with such sadness that I can't stand it."

At that thought, she wondered if she should have been honest with him. Telling him she was hosting a writers' retreat kept him away, but it also sabotaged her plan to speak and be heard.

"What am I going to do with myself? How am I supposed to meet others when I can't even face my uncle?"

Z covered his muzzle with his paw, but she still

saw the beautiful blue of his eyes. With her mother being a veterinarian, there were always animals around the house. Most days, it was like a zoo. When she moved out on her own, she could only have one pet, so she chose the Malamute. He was fierce-looking when he wanted to be, but he was all marshmallow and cream deep inside.

She turned on an oldies music channel and listened to Otis Redding singing about tenderness.

"I was born in the wrong era, Z." She was always drawn to the music of the fifties and sixties. The blues were her favorites. She could turn on the music and dance for hours by herself.

As she wound through the mountain road toward a new beginning, she kept the music playing. Up ahead, she saw a man standing on the side of the road. From what she could see, he was dressed in camouflage pants and carried a rucksack.

Just as she approached, the next song came on, and the volume rose as "Stop in the Name of Love" nearly screamed at her. She was so startled that she slammed on the brakes and came to a stop beside the man.

"What now?" She hadn't planned on picking up a hitchhiker.

The man walked over to the car, and Z popped up to look out the window. He was wary of strangers. It was probably a learned behavior he got from her.

Whenever she took him for a walk, she avoided people, even crossing the street to ensure there wasn't any interaction.

The voice in her head said, "Open the window, open your life." She knew it was her subconscious telling her to get on with her new plan.

She took a good look at him to make sure he didn't seem like a serial killer. She had no idea if there was a profile for people who murdered at will.

He had brown hair and brown eyes—eyes that didn't look dangerous but sad. His green jacket had a nametag sewn on the pocket that read Fearless. Was that another omen? One that said she should be fearless? Inside his pocket was a pink envelope peeking out. Was it a Dear John letter from a lost love? There went her writer's brain, already making up his story without a word.

He looked at her with confusion, and rightly so. She'd stopped for a hitchhiker and hadn't even spoken a word to the man. Her car idled next to him with her window closed.

Before she chickened out, she cracked the window a little and smiled. Sometimes a smile spoke the words she didn't have to.

"Thanks for stopping."

Z stuck his nose to the crack in the window and tried to lick the man. It was odd for him, but maybe he was lonely too and needed more than her.

She nodded and kept smiling.

He didn't seem to notice that she hadn't said a word.

"Hey, boy," the man said, sliding a couple of fingers inside the window to stroke Z's soft ear. "I'm heading to Aspen Cove." He stood and nodded north. "I'd appreciate a ride if you're up for some company."

Inside, she knew it was now or never, so she nodded while she unlocked the doors. She pointed to the back seat and said, "Z." He was an intuitive dog. And because she didn't speak much, he learned to follow her hand signals. Too bad people weren't as perceptive.

The man pointed to his duffel bag. "Back seat or trunk?"

She popped the trunk and waited for him to situate his belongings and take his place in the passenger seat.

When he did, he smiled warmly and said, "I'm Brandon. Thanks for the lift."

She put the car in drive and pulled back onto the highway.

"R-Reese," she said.

The first word was out, and it wasn't too painful. A minor blip, but all in all, a good start.

"Where are you headed?" he asked.

She took a deep breath and willed herself to speak clearly.

"Aspen C-c-c-c." She shook her head and wanted to crawl beneath her seat.

He nodded. "Same as me. Cool. As I said, I appreciate the ride." He adjusted his seat so his knees weren't touching the dash. "I don't want to seem ungrateful, but would you mind if I took a little siesta? I've been thumbing it since I left Texas several days ago, and I'm beat."

She shook her head.

He leaned his seat farther back. Far enough for Z to lay his head on the head rest by Brandon. "Crank up the music if you want. I've slept through worse."

She wasn't sure if he meant the noise or her taste in tunes. The oldies were still playing in the background with Dinah Shore's "What a Diff'rence a Day Makes." It was her Grandma Mae's favorite song.

She turned it up and listened to words about hope and the end of loneliness. Somehow, it all seemed fitting. It was as if the universe had created a playlist just for her.

Although she wasn't talking to Brandon, she had, and she'd survived it. Some might say she was still alone, but a glance at the man who was already asleep proved she wasn't. Just his presence made her feel less lonely.

She drove through the winding mountain pass and admired the scenery. Nature had it right. There was a tall pine nestled next to a sparsely leafed aspen. From the crack of a giant boulder grew a tiny purple flower. Differences shouldn't set us apart but give us a reason to come together. One's weakness could quickly become another's strength. The tall pine protected the tiny aspen and the fragile flower gave beauty to the rigid stone.

The last fifty minutes of her trip were spent in hopeful reflection and making side glances at the handsome drifter who managed to hitchhike to Aspen Cove from Texas. She wanted to know his story—wanted to know what that pink envelope he placed his hand protectively over the whole ride meant to him.

She pulled in front of The Corner Store and parked. It was the first stop on her journey and the last stop for theirs together.

She reached over and tapped his shoulder, and he nearly flew out of his seat. She jumped back and hit her head on the window.

"Shit ..." He shook his head. "I mean shoot. I'm sorry."

She rubbed at the spot on her head that now ached. "It's okay. I'm fine."

He frowned. "That's what we all say, but are we ever truly fine?"

OTHER BOOKS BY KELLY COLLINS

An Aspen Cove Romance Series

One Hundred Reasons

One Hundred Heartbeats

One Hundred Wishes

One Hundred Promises

One Hundred Excuses

One Hundred Christmas Kisses

One Hundred Lifetimes

One Hundred Ways

One Hundred Goodbyes

One Hundred Secrets

One Hundred Regrets

One Hundred Choices

One Hundred Decisions

One Hundred Glances

One Hundred Lessons

One Hundred Mistakes

One Hundred Nights

One Hundred Whispers

One Hundred Reflections

One Hundred Chances

One Hundred Dreams

GET A FREE BOOK.

Go to www.authorkellycollins.com

ABOUT THE AUTHOR

International bestselling author of more than thirty novels, Kelly Collins writes with the intention of keeping love alive. Always a romantic, she blends real-life events with her vivid imagination to create characters and stories that lovers of contemporary romance, new adult, and romantic suspense will return to again and again.

For More Information
www.authorkellycollins.com
kelly@authorkellycollins.com